# Roxanne and the Healer

# Roxanne and the Healer

## Carmela Haynes

WestBow
PRESS
A DIVISION OF THOMAS NELSON

WestBow Press books may be ordered through booksellers or by contacting:

WestBow Press
A Division of Thomas Nelson
1663 Liberty Drive
Bloomington, IN 47403
www.westbowpress.com
1-(866) 928-1240

Because of the dynamic nature of the Internet, any web addresses or links contained in
this book may have changed since publication and may no longer be valid. The views
expressed in this work are solely those of the author and do not necessarily reflect the views
of the publisher, and the publisher hereby disclaims any responsibility for them.

Any people depicted in stock imagery provided by Thinkstock are models,
and such images are being used for illustrative purposes only.

Certain stock imagery © Thinkstock.

Words meaning by Webster's new world dictionary; copyright 2003 by Wiley Publishing, Inc.

Some of the characters in my book are taken from God's Word, which I have
learned throughout my life, The Holy Bible, New International Version, NIV
Copyright 1973,1978,1984,2011 by Biblical Inc. was a great help.

ISBN: 978-1-4497-6699-3 (sc)
ISBN: 978-1-4497-7396-0 (e)

Library of Congress Control Number: 2012916557

Printed in the United States of America

WestBow Press rev. date: 10/31/2012

**Passion; the object of any strong desire** (Webster's dictionary)

I've often heard the comment that there are more important things to have a passion for, when I speak of my love of animals. I thought of this long and often, and I feel God spoke this revelation to my heart.

If we all had the same passions for the same one thing, say…children's needs, then there wouldn't be any one who would care for the elderly, or special needs people, sick people, blind deaf, poor or homeless people, what about caring for the dying?
If we all had the same passion for the very same need, who would care to preserve our clean air or nature, who would try to find cures for diseases and yes, who would care about the animals?
God instilled a "love" or "gift" or "talent" for something different in each of us for a reason. And he left an empty spot in our hearts for one special passion that only he can fill. With that in mind I dedicate this book to all the different passions out there who joyfully give back to our Creator. Even though it is but a small token of the greatest gift he's given us in Jesus Christ his son. For God, thru Jesus who formed us in our mothers' wombs and gave us all of our talents!

**ALL HONORS ARE HIS ALONE!**

If by reading with the eyes of one's soul, perhaps then a book's little imperfections will not show!

To my husband Dennis; Thank-you for your love and support for me and all of our Four legged family members! You have my eternal Love.

**For my children and all of my grandchildren, you all are my heart and soul,**
Never forget how much you are loved by me and more importantly by God keep him near always!

THIS IS A BOOK ABOUT PARTS OF MY LIFE.

NOT VERSES OR CHAPTERS, BUT SIMPLE LITTLE PARTS

OF A PEOPLE AND A PLACE THAT TOUCHED MY HEART.

SO I SHARE THESE LIFE PARTS NOW WITH YOU, THE

HUMANS WHO LOVE US ANIMALS SO TRUE,

I HOPE THAT THROUGH THE EYES OF THIS TALE,

YOU WILL SEE JUST HOW MUCH THE HEALER IS

IN LOVE WITH BOTH YOU AND ME!

ROXANNE

# PART ONE; THE BEGINNING

The sun felt warm on my fur, this was my favorite thing to do, just laying here by my momma's warm body, feeling the sun on my face. I came to be upon this earth about three months ago, seems like it's always been just mom and me. I have never seen my daddy and mom has not spoken of him much, but she has been telling me all about these humans I sometimes see. She said she had a whole family of them a long time ago but they left and never came back for her. She said she loved them dearly and can't understand why, so she is very hurt and warns me to never trust all humans. Some may be good she tells me but some deceive you and may seem good, but mean you harm! She made me promise to always listen to my instincts, they will warn you of danger, I promised her, even though I don't really know what an instinct is I suppose someday I'll learn.

Today, we had full bellies, mom found some meat thrown away in an alley, it was great! But most days she leaves me in the hills and goes to the city looking for food, sometimes she doesn't come back for a very long time and I get very worried. The city we live by has a great wall around it momma says with just a few large gates to go into and out of. Mom tells of the stories she heard when her human family would sit around and talks about how grand this place used to be before the day **they** came, and took over our country, I think I heard my mom call them Romans!! Yes! I believe I would be happy to stay like this forever, by my mom, in the sun, without a care in the world.

It's starting to get dark again and the weather is cold and windy. I haven't seen mom for three dark nights! She left one day to go to the city for food and hasn't been back yet! I'm hungry, cold and very scared, mom where are you? Please come home!!

# PART TWO; THE HUMAN

Adam was a kind young man, doing whatever he could to survive these harsh times. His parents had died when he was very young and left him only one possession; a beautiful blanket, which his mother had made for him when he was first born. It was blue "to match your eyes" his mother used to tell him, with white trim and sewn onto it, across the top, were the words "FOR YOU MY SWEET BABY BOY". Adam loved that little blanket and took good care of it, until someone else he met needed it more, so he gave it to him, when Adam himself was still but a small boy. A very selfless gesture, from a poor boy to an equally as poor child.

This winter had been particularly hard for him and it was still early in the year. Adam had no actual home to speak of, so he called the sky his blanket and the earth his pillow. Being that he was not the type to beg; one might say at times he was a little too prideful. He learned early on that there was usually a price attached to every gift or handout given him, and he would just be better off not owing anyone a single thing, for this reason, Adam was very determined to work, or sing (his voice was heaven sent) or do whatever he could to acquire his food and other necessity's, only going into the city when necessary. He preferred the quiet of the country and hills.

The streets were full of people, "I hate crowds" he mumbled to himself, "so hard to find work with so many in need and these solders there everywhere"! It was early morning and there was a chill in the air as he made his way through the huge gates and towards the heart of the city, Adam couldn't help but admire the spectacular wall that surrounded the whole city, this is something else, he thought, I have never seen a wall such as this, a city all by itself, perhaps this city will bring me good fortune, maybe even make a good home for me! Yes, he smiled to himself, there is something very

2

special about this place, something very special for sur...."Look out you peasant" shouted a voice from behind him, causing Adam to turn around very quickly just in time to move out of the way of six very large, very fast moving horses, which were pulling a huge chariot and upon the chariot was a large mean looking Roman solder! As he turned, he saw out of the corner of his eye and just out of his reach, a small dog running very fast, right in the path of the horses hoofs! As the dog ran past him, he reached out and tried to grab it, but he was just not fast enough, and that chariot with it's horses and Roman solder, rolled right over that poor dog, and then it just kept on going, never looking back once, like it didn't cause any harm at all. It happened so fast that by the time Adam had recovered, the dog was dragging its poor dying body towards the city's gate, almost with a purpose or urgency about it. Like it needed to be somewhere else more important and strangely it was still holding something tightly in its mouth! It was the saddest, yet strangest thing that Adam had seen in a long time, what could be so important to hold on to after being hurt like that? He wondered. Well I can't watch this poor animal suffer anymore, Adam said, and since everyone else around was just going about their business like nothing ever happened, he walked over to get an idea of how badly the animal was hurt. He saw that it was a girl dog, and very beautiful, black, white and a little brown, and on the top of the head was a black spot in the shape of a heart! It looked like she had puppies recently; her belly was still somewhat saggy from that. Adam placed his hand softly upon her head, she looked at him as if she had something important to tell him, but all she could do was put a paw on his hand, and then she drew her last breath and died. There was something about helpless innocence that always would touch Adam's heart. He just hated to see animals or children or old people suffer. And this little girl, well it just wasn't right, what happened to her. "I'll take her to the hills and bury her by the flowers and trees" he mumbled to himself. So slowly and with great tenderness, Adam picked her up, and put her over his shoulder, it was then that she finally let go of the mouthful of meat that she still had clutched in her jaws, he watched as it fell to the dusty earth, not knowing why it was of such importance to her. As he headed outside the city's gates and towards the hills, all his earlier joy for the day was now gone, along with the hope of finding a home.

# PART THREE; MISUNDERSTOOD

What should I do? My mom hasn't come back! I'm cold, hungry and scared! Wait, I see something! What's that coming up the hill? Is it mommy? Oh please be mommy, I can't quite see--little too far away--- too dark to make out, oh nooo it's one of those human things!! What's it doing way out here and what's that on its shoulders? I wonder if it's one of the good ones. Suppose if it's seen my mom, maybe if it is one of those good ones mamma would talk about. Maybe if I get closer my instincts will let me know.

Adam heard a snap of a twig and a rustling of a bush; he came to a dead stop. Who's in there! He bellowed, with as much menacing voice as he could muster up. But no one spoke, just the sound of the wind thru the olive trees. Shrugging his shoulders he gently placed the lady dog on the ground as if she was still alive, and he didn't want to hurt her. There it is again! Walking closer towards the bush he picked up a stick, just in case it was a wild animal or something. Bellowing again he shouted "Come out now or I'll come and get you", nothing "if I have to go over there I promise it won't be pretty"!! The bush parted, he raised his stick just in case, it was then he heard the faintest whimper and saw this little black, white and brown puppy emerge from the bush, dropping the stick and using a gentler voice, he cooed, come here fella, I won't hurt you. As the pup drew closer, sniffing furiously at the air, trying to determine if he was a threat or not Adam figured, "come here" Adam cooed again, and again the pup came a little closer, now he could see something very familiar on this animal, A spot, right on the top of the head, in the shape of a perfect heart! Adam picked up the pup very slowly, it seemed very frightened. Well you're no bigger than a fig, what are you doing way out here all alone? Then Adam remembered the girl dog that had been run over, why you must be her baby, that heart on your head is perfect match to your momma's. She must have been trying to get back to you little uh... you a boy or girl? Adam slowly turned the pup around why you're a girl! He exclaimed. What do you think about giving you a name? Let me see, I always liked the name Roxanne that was my mother's name. What do you think about that? Do you like the name Roxanne? Just then she gave Adam a big lick, right on his cheek, ok, ok, he laughed, Roxanne it is! Now you stay here and wait, there's something I need to finish, and I don't want you to see what it is. SO STAY! He pointed a finger at her and set her on the ground don't move Roxanne. Then he quickly turned and went down the hill to where he left her mother.

Roxanne sat as the man walked a few feet down the hill and started to dig a hole. Well, I know it told me not to move but I can't see a thing from here she thought, I'll just inch a little closer in and take a peek at what it's doing, what is he picking up? Wait, what's that scent? Why does that smell so familiar.... then Roxanne's eyes lit up, why it's... before she could think of what Adam told her to not do, her little legs had her running towards that scent she knew so well, and right to where Adam was doing whatever he was that he didn't want her to see. I'll just get this hole dug a little deeper bury mamma and we will be on our way Adam said to himself. He was so busy digging he didn't hear her running up from behind him, then he turned at a noise he heard, and saw her running full speed towards him and her dead momma. STAY!! Adam yelled don't come any closer! But all Roxanne knew was that her mom was near, as she got closer she stopped, almost running into Adams legs that were now a few inches in between her and her mom. Go Back! Adam demanded, trying to sound angry. Roxanne neither heard him nor cared; all she could see now is her mom's lifeless body, lying on the ground and a big stick in Adams hand with some kind of scoop on the end of it. As she went closer she saw the blood on her mom, and finally noticed Adam. It was then that Roxanne's mother's words came back to her..."Men can appear to be nice but mean you great harm!" She looked at Adam then at her mom, and at Adam again, her eyes accusing him of the wrong that lay before her. No! Adam said, seeing the hurt in her eyes, no Roxanne, I didn't hurt her! But all Roxanne could see or hear was her own pain, so she ran barley hearing Adam yelling after her to stop. Roxanne ran and ran till she thought her heart would burst, the picture of her mom lying there dead, haunting her every step! Why, why would anyone do that, why hurt my mom? I don't understand, I thought that one was one of the nice ones! What will happen to me now? I'm all alone. More afraid than ever before, Roxanne ran so fast and hard she barely noticed the big gates, the huge walls surrounding the city, or all the people around, especially Adam, who was running fast and hard trying to catch up with her. Suddenly, she heard a whinny, a sound like thunder, and what she thinks was loud cries from her own throat, then nothing.....sweet peace, quiet, and no more pain, just darkness.

# PART FOUR; ENCOUNTERS

LOOK OUT!!! Adam yelled, but Roxanne was oblivious, she just kept running. That awful sound! The thud! No, No not again, he screamed, but it was too late by the time he caught up to Roxanne, she had already ran into the road, right in front of a horse pulling a wagon. This wagon, at least took the time to actually stop even if only for a moment, they looked at her lying there unmoving, the dog's dead, let's go before the solders get here! Then off they went leaving Roxanne in the road, lifeless and alone. Roxanne! Yelled Adam, please get up! As he furiously rubbed her side trying anything to get her to open her eyes or even to take a breath, both which was not happening! Adam did not even notice the young man standing in front of him and Roxanne. What happened, he asked? Adam didn't even look up; he just kept rubbing Roxanne's side and looking down at her. The young man kneeled down to get a closer look. Is she dead, he asked? Adam just could not bring himself to say the actual words, so he just shook his head. When Adam finally looked up at the young man, he looked into the most compassionate and caring, and yes even little haunting, eyes that he had ever seen. So full of love they were, that it startled Adam for a brief moment, yes, Adam finally answered the strangers question, barley hearing himself speaks, she is, and it's my entire fault! The young man touched the pup," look here" he said, why she's not dead! Only sleeping! See she's breathing!! Adam looked down and saw Roxanne's chest move up and down, amazed he just stared at the young man, then back at Roxanne, he could hardly believe what he was seeing. Her leg is hurt, stated this young fellow, she'll need your care, but I think she will be fine, he told Adam all the while smiling. Just then someone called for him, and before Adam was done processing what just took place, he looked up, and the young man was gone! Wait! Adam yelled into the crowd, I didn't get to thank-you, who are you? What's your name? Looking all around Adam could not see that fellow again. Just then he heard a small whimper, Whhat happened? Why is my leg hurting so bad, she tried to cry out but all she could manage is a small whine, and to open her eyes, and there before her was that human, with his own tears of spilling down his face. Perhaps, she thought, this is a good human after all.

As carefully as possible, Adam picked up Roxanne and carried her to the nearest place, a stable, please he pleaded with the blacksmith who happened to own the place, and may we stay here till my dog is better? I'll work for our food and board, I'll care for her myself, I'll even sleep out here with my dog, please he begged again, I haven't anywhere else to go. The owner looked at Adam and Roxanne and took pity on them; he too loved animals, so he agreed. Roxanne's front left leg was very bad, broken and cut, but other than that all else seemed ok. It's a miracle Adam thought. I swear that she was dead, that wagon rolled right over her middle! I know she wasn't breathing! Roxanne gave a small whine and tried to move, jolting Adam back to what he was doing. No, Roxanne stay, don't move Adam softly said, I'm going to care for you, just be calm, he started to lightly pet her face and sing a melody his own mother used to sing to him when he was scared and she fell back asleep. Quickly Adam found some clean rags and some sticks for a splint. The owner of the stable gave Adam some horse ointment that he "makes himself," he stated rather proudly, for the wound; it will help in the healing and pain. So Adam proceeded to set and wrap the leg, next he found some herbs he had in his bag, boiled them down and cooled the water, then gave it to Roxanne, this will numb the pain and help you to sleep he whispered. Don't worry little girl, I won't leave you alone. I couldn't help your mother, but I will not let you die. Roxanne heard these words. Finally she understood, that **he** didn't hurt her mom, he **is** a good human! Maybe he will be my family now. With that thought she fell into a deep, peaceful sleep.

She'll sleep for a while now; Adam said more to assure himself than to the blacksmith. He turned to the blacksmith and looked at him completely for the first time. He was quite tall, and seemed very slender for his height, his face was kind looking and very hairy, Adam tried hard not to stare at the long jagged scar over his left cheek "Thank-you for all you have done to help me and my dog", Adam stated as he held out his right arm. It felt good calling Roxanne his dog. My name is Adam. The man took Adam's forearm gripped it tightly, hello; he said my name is Simeon, and you and your dog are very welcome! Now, Adam said with a half-smile, point me in the direction where I'm needed and put me to work! Tell you what, replied Simeon, sun's going down and I'm hungry! I have some lamb stew I've been simmering all day, let's call it a day and start early tomorrow. Adam was a little hesitant to accept much more charity, (that old pride returning back), without some repayment from him first, but he sure was tired and realized that he hadn't eaten all day, what with all this drama of dogs coming back to life and all!! I kindly accept said Adam, but I want to make sure Roxanne is ok before I eat. No problem, replied Simeon, tell you what, take this stool and go sit by her, and I'll bring you out a steaming bowl of stew. Before Adam could protest, Simeon had vanished ton the little house and came out with a bowl of stew.

What is that wonderful smell? Where is it coming from, and why can't I move my leg? Roxanne forced her eyes opened and tried to get her legs to go under her. Now don't move, Adam spoke quietly, as she could focus more, her mind got clearer and her memory came rushing back, her mom lying dead, her running away, Adam, the wagon, some other person, then pain! She let out a yelp, once again Adam was there slowly picked her up and held her close, you're gonna be fine, I'll take care of you Roxanne, here try to eat some stew, it was then at that very moment that Roxanne knew with all her heart, that this human *was* a good one and her only family now.

Six months had passed since that fateful and terrible day. and Roxanne's leg had healed nicely, couldn't even tell it was even injured, except for the fact that if Roxanne tried move faster than a brisk walk she would have a limp, which became more prominent the faster she went. That didn't slow her down any especially, when it came to chasing the mice Simeon had around the stable. Roxanne would have been perfectly happy spending the rest of her life there at the stable, but she knew Adam all too well, and he had that restless look in his eyes.

Adam had worked hard for Simeon, and the two had forged a special friendship, almost a father and son type relationship. But Adam was not one to outwear a welcome, and being in the city this long was starting to get on his nerves. So he decided that he and Roxanne would move on." Sure to return again someday", he told Simeon, just need to get out of this city awhile. You have been so good to us, I hope that you understand." I understand more than you realize", go do what you need to do; I'll be here when you want to come home. Home, Adam thought to himself, I finally have a home and now I have this need to leave. Why? So just like that off they went down the dirt road, big Adam and little Roxanne trying to keep up the pace limp and all!

# PART FIVE; ADVENTURE'S BEGINNING

What is that!!!! There standing in front of Roxanne was this large and not too hairy, very long legged creature. Staring, at the two lumps on its back, Roxanne took a few steps backward and started this low growl. Still staring and growling at this thing Roxanne, (hiding just behind Adams legs of course) had grown into a fine looking dog. Her coat was shiny and long, and her eyes alert and bright and she still had that perfect black heart on top of her head. Adam and Roxanne had been on the road so to speak and inseparable. For a long time now, close to seven years. They have seen and done a lot together, no greater a bond has been formed between a man and an animal as with Roxanne and Adam, she took care of him and he of her. But **this**, was really asking too much!! Does he really expect me to get close to that thing thought as she watched in horror as Adam climbed on top of one who was kneeling down, chewing something and making weird chomping noises! "Come on Roxanne", Adam coaxed, "it's not so bad girl". Sitting upon the seat of this beast Adam tried his best to get Roxanne to come to him. Finally after it seemed like no coaxing was going to work he finally gave up, got off, and went over picked up Roxanne and put her on his lap, sat on the beast himself and up and off they went! Adam had joined a caravan to get himself back to the great city with the wall. He had come upon some travelers a few days ago who had recently been in the city. They had not only been in the city but had also been at the blacksmiths stable, repairing some items they received in another trade. Adam had told them that the owner is a good friend of his and asked how he was getting along? Well, the man had told him, but I heard there was a bad sickness going around in that area, and your blacksmith friend... well, he didn't look as if he was feeling too good. When I asked if he was felling ok, he just said he was fine and blamed it on getting old, and being a little tired. But if you ask me he was more than just tired! Why do you think that? I asked him. The man was very thin and pale he replied, seemed very weak, and he had some kind of red blotches on his arms! Adam thanked the traveler for his information; he promptly went and got set up with a caravan going out of Egypt and back to his home. He was very worried and in a hurry now more than ever to get out of this desert and back to the city and to Simeon. Roxanne, however just wanted to get off this smelly animal and be back on her own four paws again! But for now she decided to try and to relax and enjoy the view. It was quite a while before they arrived to the hills just outside the city, Roxanne knew the place well and the memories of life with her and her mother came quickly back to her mind. Adam also had some memories, pointing he said look Roxanne that is where I first found you, and there, half talking to Roxanne, half talking to himself, that garden over there would be a great place to have a house, close to the river, not real far from the city, plenty of shade, and just as he was getting ready to say something else a horrible smell over took them all--What Is That Smell!!, they all covered faces with their long turbans-Roxanne whined and buried her head in Adams lap!" I have smelled this before", said the leader of the caravan, "it's the smell of death"!! Come we must leave this place immediately! Just then, a group of very dirty people wrapped in even dirtier rags, appeared with open palms, begging for food or money. They were the source of that horrible smell and Roxanne dug her face so far into Adam's lap that she almost knocked both of them off their camel. The legs and arms of these unfortunate beggars were covered in open wounds, full of puss and infection and flies. "Please", they pleaded with open hands help us. Although Adam couldn't bear the smell much longer he also felt pity for these outcasts, knowing himself what it is like to be hungry and alone, so he stopped his camel as someone was approaching him arms outstretched. It was a child, maybe ten years or so and her mother looking like she was more dead than alive. "Please sir", my child is starving, so Adam untied his money pouch and gave all he could spare. "Bless you" she said, and then the others in the caravan saw what he did and proceeded to do the same, most staying down wind and as far away as possible from the beggars. We must leave, now cried the leader to the caravan. Everyone was more than compliant! Ready to get away from the terrible scene before them, especially Roxanne, who just spotted the small mound of dirt--where she remembered her mom, was buried. Exhausted, she just lay in Adams lap, and as they all went on the way to that great city with its huge gates and incredible wall!! We are onto our next adventure thought Roxanne; little did she know what an amazing adventure the future had in store for them both!

# PART SIX; HOME AGAIN

It was turning dust when they turned down the dirt road to their friend's house, bidding good-bye to their new found friends, Adam and Roxanne gathered up their belongings (which included only a few items of clothing for Adam, an extra pair of sandals, a cape for the rain, a wood bowel that Adam made for Roxanne to eat out of and a small leather pouch that he carried a few coins in and a small wooden horse that someone had carved for him). Gratefully Adam slid off the Camel happy to be on solid ground again, especially grateful was Roxanne! Who once she was on solid ground proceeded to walk not realizing that two of her three good legs had fallen asleep and she immediately fell right on her behind, giving everyone a good laugh! Roxanne, Adam chuckled, you have got to be the cutest dog I ever had the pleasure of loving! Here let me help you! Just as Adam was getting ready to pick up Roxanne, a very large group of people rushed past them almost knocking Adam himself off of his feet! Startled by the noise and with the memory of the chariot hitting Roxanne, still in his mind, instinctively, he grabbed Roxanne quickly and held her close to him as he turned to see what all the excitement was about. What's the big hurry! He yelled, rather sarcastically, as they ran past him and the caravan he was riding with. A woman who was running with the crowd slowed some as she ran past them and touched Adam's arm, come she said and see the prophet at the river. He is baptizing people and speaking of one who is to come after him that is going to save us all! Come all of you and be baptized! She shouted again with joy as she turned and ran to catch up with her friends who were all heading out of the city towards the river. Prophets! Hmm! Scowled Adam, never did me any good! They come and go here like the locusts, just as useful in my opinion! We have been gone from here eight years now and seems like now much has changed eh Roxanne?

"You my friend", laughed one of Adams traveling companions, as he slapped Adam on the shoulder "are way too young to be so cynical"! "Have you not heard of the ancient ones talk of a great king arriving someday and bringing with him peace and hope? But I guess till then we look for answers in the stars eh my friend? Well it's time for me to leave you to your destiny now; you take care of yourself and your little dog too! I will Adam said, rather loudly, as they pulled away and thank-you for all of your kindness, take care of yourself and be safe! Adam watched a long time as they got smaller and smaller in the distance, well ole' girl he finally said to Roxanne who was fast asleep by his feet, let's get on home to Simeon, I'm sure he's waiting for us. It's about time, she jumped to her feet, and the faster Roxanne got away from those smelly beasts the better, as far as she was concerned! With that off they went down the familiar dirt road that they traveled on when they left eight years ago. As Adam and Roxanne proceeded down the dirt road, they walked faster and faster the closer they got to the Black Smith shop. I am really looking forward to spending time with Simeon, Adam said, how about you Roxanne? Are you ready to stay in one place for a while? Roxanne just barked! And Adam laughed! As they approached the path to Simeon's shop it was familiar to both of them even though it was getting to be early evening. Were just about their ol' girl Adam said rather tiredly, Roxanne just whined a little whine very tired herself, then as they turned the corner up to the walkway, she suddenly darted ahead of Adam barking furiously and leaping into the dark air! I thought I recognized that bark, a familiar voice rang out in the darkness! Well old man I hope you caught her, don't want to have to fix another broken leg! Adam said with an ear to ear smile on his face. To be sure said Simeon, I am not yet that old!! Simeon! My friend Adam cried as he finally reached the fire light of the shop! Adam! The two hugged squishing Roxanne between them, she let out a whimper! Sorry girl Simeon said, it's sure good to see you to he laughed! Took you two long enough to come home, stated Simeon. Yea well busy place here this city, ran into lots of crowds, yelling something about prophets and so on, you know how it is. Oh yes Simeon said, this place is crawling with them, me I'm waiting for the true one to come. And I know one day he will! Now come inside,

I've been holding supper for you two. So they all went inside together, smells wonderful, Adam said, Roxanne agreed! As soon as Simeon lit up the room with the oil lamp, Adam could see the huge difference in him that he didn't notice outside in the dark, and it took all he had to hold back the look of shock that he felt inside. He was very thin and pale, yet there were red blotches all over his skin like when you have a very high fever. The smile left Adam's face, you feeling ok? He asked. Fine, Fine Simeon lied, just a little tired, now let's eat, it's getting cold! Adam looked at Roxanne as he put a bowel of food down for her, I don't think he's ok at all girl, he whispered, with a very worried look on his face, let's keep a close eye on him ok? Roxanne could only wag her tail, because her nose was deep into her bowel, eating!!

# PART SEVEN; FRIENDS

T he next few days went by pretty fast for Adam, the Blacksmith shop was quite busy, and Adam was helping out as best as he could with the little knowledge the he had on blacksmithing, he managed to watch and pick-up the rest pretty quickly, trying to take some of the overload so Simeon wouldn't get so tired. As time went on and things got to calm down some, Adam thought Simeon could get a chance to rest, and maybe tend to those sores that had erupted on his skin. Seemed like no matter what home remedy they tried, they just got worse, and seemed like they were spreading quite fast. Adam didn't say anything to but they almost looked like the same thing those beggars had outside of town. No! He thought to himself, dismissing even the idea of this being more than a mild annoyance of a rash, all Simeon needed is some time to relax and get well, and I'm going to give it to him! And that is exactly what Adam did, working well into the night, sometimes seven days a week, doing it all, so Simeon could take it easy, but he just got weaker and weaker and the sores got redder and more infected, spreading to most parts of his body, eating away at his flesh. Already up in his years, and not in the best of health before all this happened, seemed to enable this illness to progress more quickly than Adam had expected. I'm afraid old girl Adam said to Roxanne, as he was petting her one especially hard day, that we are going to lose our dear friend. I just don't know what else more I can do for him. Roxanne saw the sadness in Adams eyes-remembering the sadness of losing her own mom, she just gave Adam a lick on the hand and curled up in his lap, as if to say "I love you and you're not alone". Suddenly Adam was jolted out of his thoughts back into the present by a strong and loud cry from Simeon! Jumping up he practically knocked Roxanne onto the floor, grabbing her at the last minute, sorry girl, he stated as he set her on the floor. Simeon! Adam yelled are you ok? No answer. Simeon! He yelled again as he ran towards the bedroom, when he entered there was Simeon on the floor crying and holding something in his hand. Simeon, Adam said very softly, what's the matter? What's wrong? Please, he pleaded, you're scaring me, finally Adam got down on the floor with him, Simeon look up, with the most horrified, sad, confused, look that Adam ever saw, what is happening to me Adam? Look, he lifted up his hand and opened it, inside was the tip of his left pinky! Adam gasped! It just fell off when I went to scratch my face Simeon said, and it didn't even hurt! Adam grabbed a cloth nearby and took the fingertip out of Simon's hand, come-on he said; let me get you back to your bed. After Adam got Simeon up and settled and finished wrapping his hand with a bandage, he sat there awhile to make sure he was ok, not knowing what else to do or say. Tell me some stories of you and Roxanne's adventures, when you were one the road traveling these past seven years, maybe it will keep my mind off of my body parts rotting off! With that he smiled for the first time in a while, which caused Adam to do the same," very funny", Adam replied. Let me see, what adventure do you think should I talk about first, Roxanne? Would you like to hear about the time Roxanne came face to face with a wild boar? Or how about the time when we were in Egypt and she climbed a pyramid and go stuck at the top and couldn't get down? I know! I'll tell you about the time we had to spend the night out in the desert. It was not long after we left here, on the way to Egypt; well I got the bright idea to cut our travel time, by going into the desert wilderness!! Oh no Adam! Simeon said you didn't! Oh yes I did! So out we went, just me Roxanne and our horse, on what I thought was enough water, it wasn't long before I realized just how wrong I was. Let me tell you Simeon, Adam said as he leaned in a little closer towards Simeon, I never in my life seen a sand storm come up so fast and so huge as that one. One minute Roxanne and I were just riding along, and the next I hear this strange deafening noise, like a thousand horses running all at once! Roxanne was the first to look behind us, never heard her make such a loud whine before, made me turn and look, before I had the time to get off that horse and get my footing, she was running past me. I yelled at her to stop but the noise of the storm was too loud, it just drowned out my words and carried them away with the wind. What did you do? Asked Simeon, who now was sitting up in his bed, eyes wide with interest. I didn't know what to do other than run in the same direction that she ran. So I did, as fast and as hard as I could, calling Roxanne's name all the while. I saw this small cave ahead, so I ran inside hoping she did the same, just missing being over taken by the huge sand wall! Was Roxanne in there, asked Simeon? No, said Adam as he looked at Roxanne almost as if she wasn't here sitting on the end of the bed. I laid down at the mouth of that cave yelling her name over and over till I lost my voice, I swallowed enough sand, I thought I was going to vomit! Still I kept calling, till I fell asleep, or passed out, I'm not sure which. By the time I woke up, I was covered in sand, but I was alive, and the sky was clear! I had lost everything; the horse had run off somewhere, I had only a small amount of water left and no Roxanne to be found anywhere! Without a clue as to which way to go or even where to look I set out on foot, hoping to see some kind of clue as to where she was. Seemed like I walked forever, then all of a sudden a boy appeared, from out of nowhere; "you lose a dog" he asked? I just stood there, my mouth opened, staring, like some fool, he asked again. "Hey brother," did you lose a dog"? Yes! I finally managed to spit out of my mouth. Have you seen her? Well that's a dumb question, Simeon blurted out! Of course he's seen her; why else would he be asking that, in the middle of a desert after a sand storm! Do you want to hear the rest of this story or just make some more fun of me? Adam asked with a smile on his face. OK Ok, Simeon said continue, sheesh you sure are touchy lately! Now where was I, oh yea the boy appearing out of thin air, he told me "your dog is safe", she's waiting for you back there. So off we went, me and this boy or should I say young man, it wasn't long before I heard that familiar bark I've grown so used to and the next thing I knew she was in my arms, giving me a tongue bath! I have to tell you Simeon, when I woke up in that cave and no Roxanne around, I was so scared, I didn't know what to think, I would never have forgiven myself if something bad would have happened to her, because of my dumb idea, to go by way of the desert, Adam said as he picked up Roxanne and she settled herself quite comfortable in his lap, anyway, back to the desert. After our happy reunion, this young man invited us to stay the night. I was getting to be dusk now and the sun was setting and the desert air was starting to cool, so I agreed. The cave he took us to was not very large, but it was big enough for us to stand and move around and build a small fire in. As we sat around the fire, I finally felt relaxed enough to take a good look at this mysterious fellow that saved both Roxanne's and my lives. He was tall, I'd say about leaving his boyhood and entering young manhood, he wore a camel skin only and he had this wild look in his eyes, yet there also was a look of kindness and peace, and wait till I tell you what he offered us to eat! What, exclaimed Simeon! I'll get to that, be patient Adam teased! Anyway, there we were sitting around the fire, me, Roxanne, and this fellow, all of us tired, and very quiet. By the way, my name is Adam, I said breaking the awkward silence, and this little rascal is Roxanne! Shalom, my name is John, he told me, and shalom to you too Roxanne he said. So John, do you live out here, I asked? No, I live in a small town outside of Jerusalem. I come out here often to reflect on things. Oh, I said, I guess then you know your way around here pretty well then. Oh yes, he said, say I bet you two are pretty hungry aren't you? That was all Roxanne needed to hear, she sat up and started to bark and carry on, well I said I guess it has been awhile since we've eaten. Be right back he said, and off he went to the back of the cave. A few minutes later he returned with two plates one with some honey and another with freshly killed slightly cooked locusts!!! What, are you kidding exclaimed Simeon! Nope it's the truth, said Adam. So, there we were, watching this strange man who without his help, both of us probably would have died. Put a big helping of locust first then pour honey over it, and then set that plate in front of Roxanne! I thought she was going to pass out right there! Simeon couldn't contain himself any longer he just let out a huge laugh and couldn't stop. She must have had the funniest look on her face; she is the pickiest eater, for a pup, I have ever met. Adam looked at Simeon for a moment, it sure is good to see him smile again, Adam thought, he seems to be getting so weak so fast now. Continue, said Simeon, I can't wait to hear how you got out of this eating situation. Well, Adam said, when he put that plate of locusts in front of me all smothered in honey, I politely asked him if he wouldn't mind looking outside of the cave and see if the storm had passed, and when he walked to the mouth of the cave I quickly dug a little hole with Roxanne helping of course, and dumped both plates in the hole and covered it up before he came back, just in the nick of time I might add! Very clever, you two, Simeon chimed in then what? Then he came back and sat down and got this strange faraway look in his eyes and started talking about someone who was coming very near in the future who would have all the answers of our hearts and will save the world from its own destruction. Someone who is greater than anyone who has ever been or will ever be and he John is to the fore runner, the announcer for this person, to prepare people for his arrival! So what did you make of all that? Simeon asked. You know me, Adam said, I'm not one to go all crazy about these so called prophets, there are so many of them too hard to tell the real from the fake, but this time was different, this man, no, this boy was so convincing, and the look on his face,,, and his eyes... well, let's just say I'm not so quick to judge anymore, and it would be real interesting to meet this so called savior of the world and look into his eyes. Anyway there we were deep in conversation one minute the storm really out of control, and then the next minute he stands up, says "storms over time to go". Just like that! Asked Simeon. Just like that! Adam said. So I picked up Roxanne, and followed him out of the cave, hoping he really knew the way out, it seemed like we walked forever and just as I was starting to doubt-- a small town appeared, to my and Roxanne's relief!! I turned around to let our friend know that I spotted a town and he was gone! Gone! Simeon echoed. Yes, gone! As in disappeared! Nowhere to be found, I didn't even get to thank him. So there was nothing else to do but go to the town. And that's how Roxanne and I came out of what could of been our deaths in the wilderness! What a great story! Simeon shook his head and whistled! Now, Adam said as he stood up it's time for you to get some rest! Ok, ok I really enjoyed that story, Adam thanks for the adventure. Hey! Got anymore? I would love to hear another one! Do I have anymore! As he got up snickering, why that is just the tip of the top of a very large mountain! Do I have any more he asks! You bet I do! But for now my friend gets some sleep it's late! Adam made his way towards the door, Thanks again, Simeon said Adam, turned towards him and asked for what? For coming home, for all your help, for being the son I never had. Well... Adam said softly, choking back a tear, your welcome, and he picked up Roxanne, good night Simeon, and with that he left Simeon alone.

Lying in the bed that night, Adam thought about his life, and all the adventures he and Roxanne have had these past seven years. We sure have had us a time, haven't' we girl, he stated as he lifted her up onto his bed, petting her head and drifting into the past, I remember the time when you insisted upon climbing that half-done Pyramid, chasing after that darn cat only to find yourself stuck at the top, and afraid to move! Never heard you make that howl before, sure took a lot of climbing and some bribing of Egyptian authorities to convince them to let me get you down. I think that you were never so happy Adam said, with a chuckle in his voice, as you were to see my face or be on solid ground again as you were that day, were you girl? Roxanne, looking up gave Adam a very serious look, as if to say that she did not approve of his chuckle of such a serious and scary time in her life! Yes, we sure have had us some adventures haven't we? Just as Adam was starting to drift off to a peaceful sleep, Roxanne started a low menacing growl, bringing Adam back to the present, and on alert. What's the matter girl what do you hear? Then as if on cue the peaceful quiet of the night gave way to the sound of banging on the door! Bam Bam Bam!!! Open up! What's going on? Simeon's frail and slightly confused sounding voice asked from his bed in his room? I don't know replied Adam, stay there! I'll go and see. As Adam got closer to the front door he could make out what looked like torches and a mob of people. Bam Bam the door gave way to the pounding on the other side again. Open up or I'll break it down!! A faceless voice yelled from the other side. Who are you, and what do you want? Adam yelled, above the frantic barking of Roxanne. We are solders of the Emperor, and we order everyone here to leave this place immediately! You're what?! Exclaimed Adam as he threw open the door and came face to face with two very large very angry looking Roman soldiers, carrying swords and torches, and behind them, what looked like to be the city's high council, or something like that, and behind them, lots of very angry looking people. What is all this about? Adam asked, a little bit softer this time. By order of the council and the governor of this providence, you and your entire household are hereby ordered to vacate this house immediately, to be banned from this town, and not to be within 30 feet of its city walls, or from the gate's entrance! For a moment, Adam just stood there, staring, finally he just asked, but why? What have we done? We haven't broken any laws, besides I have a very sick man inside, and he can't be moved, if he is forced to, he will surely die! Just then, Simeon called out from the darkness of his room. Adam, is everything o.k.? Everything is fine Simeon. Adam called back to the darkness, it's just a small misunderstanding, don't worry, go back to bed. Simeon started to turn around when one of the solders yelled, hey you in the room, what's wrong with you? Oh, Simeon replied, just old and tired I guess, why? Come out here, we want to take a look at you! As Simeon stepped into the light of their torches all it took was one look at the open sores on Simeon's face and arms, and that alone sent the crowd into a frenzy! Yelling at Simeon UNCLEAN! UNCLEAN!!! You have the marks of sinners, you leave now or die!!! All the while covering their faces with their wraps, afraid to breathe the same air as Simeon, as if he was some hideous monster in front of them, instead of a man in need of care. Stunned, Adam wasn't sure what to make of all of this, but one thing was sure, if he didn't get Simeon out, and out fast, neither one of them would see the light of day! ALRIGHT! He yelled, over the angry mob, were leaving!! Just give us some time to get some things together! You have ten minutes! Said the solders, then you're dead! Adam turned to Simeon, gather what you can, he said quietly, and I'll get the rest of what I can. Come on Roxanne, we don't have much time. With that Adam started to get some blankets and what dried meat he could find, some bread, and anything else he thought he could use to try and make Simeon and Roxanne as comfortable as possible wherever they ended up. Simeon appeared in the doorway of the little room where Adam was trying to gather as many blankets and items that he could think of and put them in a basket, "why are they doing this Adam"?, Simeon asked. I don't know, my friend, Adam replied, but I do know one thing, if we stay here, were dead, so let's go ok! Do you have everything you need in that sack? Yea, replied Simeon, very sadly. Slowly, Adam opened the front door, instructing Roxanne to stay close to him he noticed only the solders and the few council members remained outside, the mob had moved back down the dirt road but still stood by waiting to make sure that the job was done to their satisfaction. As Adam, Simeon and Roxanne stepped out into the night air, people acted as though they were afraid of them, keeping well away from them and turning away as they walked by as if to wipe them clean away from ever existing .By the time they got to the big gates, no one but the soldiers were left outside the gate far off, there were some torch lights that Adam could see. Not knowing what else to do or where else to go, he picked up Roxanne, and with her under one arm, and helping Simeon walk with the other, and having the basket tied to his back, Adam headed towards the light, feeling like he had the burden of the whole world on his shoulders, but determined to find someone or somewhere to take care of Simeon and hoping that the light was the way.

# PART EIGHT; HARDSHIPS

Roxanne wriggled, she was very uncomfortable, closing her eyes she dreamt about her place at the end of Adam's bed, soft and warm and what seemed to be so long ago an actual home. Now here they are, in the hills on another adventure! Only this one is not so much fun. Since that awful night that they got forced out of their home, it's been very hard. For some reason, to which she cannot understand no one has been very helpful or even a little nice towards any of them or even very nice for that matter. Everyone runs away from them when they come near, and the only ones that were even a little nice were the people they saw that first night they left their home and Adam led them all towards that light, Roxanne adjusted herself on the thin shirt and hay-bed that Adam had made for her trying to get herself a little more comfortable. As she looked at Adam and Simeon sleeping nearby, she could see Simeon's face in the firelight, looking and smelling more and more like those people that were there by the light that first night without their home. Hold on Simeon! Adam had pleaded it's not very far to those torches; I think that they are waiting for us; they don't seem to be getting any dimmer! The closer they got, the stronger the smell, whining Roxanne half jumped, half was dropped from Adam's arms, following her master as far back as possible she, cautiously, went closer to those torches and that smell grew stronger and stronger the closer they got. Suddenly! Adam yelled her name Roxanne!!! Without a second thought Roxanne took off running to Adam's side, the placing herself in front of him and whatever was holding those torches, growling and barring her teeth! A group of people had surrounded them feeling threatened for her masters safety she tried her best to look threating and dangerous~!But the minute she saw one of the faces clearly in the light of the torch, she ran crying loudly, directly behind Adam's and Simeon's legs and hid, doing something between a growl-whine!" I apologize", said a voice behind the torch, I didn't mean to scare your dog so badly. Who are you people? Adam asked, as he adjusted Simeon's arm and body to better support him. We are the forgotten, the unwanted, and the diseased outcasts of this city, the same as you two! What are you talking about! Adam protested with more anger than he intended, I have nothing in common with you people!! Maybe not yet, the voice said, but your friend does, and you soon will! The fire crackled loudly and brought Roxanne back to the present, looking over at Simeon and shuddering at how angry Adam had been that fateful night, she had never been afraid of him, except for that first day in the hills when they first met and she thought that he had killed her momma. But when they had told him that Simeon was just like them, well let's just say Adam got so angry that he picked her up gathered Simeon tighter and just pushed right thought those people like they were not even there! And he kept on walking not slowing down once even to answer the voice calling out... You're just like us! The voice kept yelling out, you'll see, those sores. They spread! They kill!! Violent coughing caused Roxanne to move from where she was lying and go over to check on Simeon, looking at him now sleeping, she sat down by his side. What's the matter girl? Adam asked, as he came up behind her, sitting on the ground he put her in his lap, are you having trouble sleeping? Roxanne looked at Simeon, then up at Adam, with worries in her eyes, I know girl, he said very sadly time is getting short isn't it? Come on let's try and get some sleep, tomorrow's another long day. Roxanne curled up beside her friend and closed her eyes, both thinking the same thought; that faceless voice calling out in the dark saying "your friend does have the same thing in common with us and soon so will you!!

# PART NINE; HOPE

The sun was high in the sky with the threat of a pending storm, when Adam reached the great city's gate. He had left Roxanne back in the hills to watch over Simeon, while he went into the city for supplies. Simeon had but a precious few days left now and Adam wanted to make them as happy and as comfortable as he possible could. He thought if he could get some things to make his last days, more bearable, then maybe he himself could bear Simeon's death. Not that he had much money to spare but he wanted to do something other than sit there and watch him suffer. The city was crowed as usual, but Adam knew just what he wanted to get. He wanted to make Simeon's favorite soup for him, so he needed to buy the ingredients for that and he wanted to get something to help soothe all those sores he had on him. After he had purchased all the items he needed, he decided to go and see about the smithy shop. Just as he turned the corner to go check on Simeon's place, his mouth opened wide in astonishment at what was before him! What happened! He said to no one but himself, the closer he got to the blacksmith's stable the more Adam's eyes stared in disbelief. Standing now directly in front of the only home he ever had he exclaimed in a loud voice "What Happened Here!" Looking at what used to be a very useful stable was now nothing but a few pieces of charred wood! The whole blacksmith shop had been burned to the ground, and Simeon's humble home, gone also, along with everything that they had left inside. A stranger walking by had seen Adam standing there, still holding all his supplies with this look of part bewilderment, part anger on his face. Shalom, said the stranger, Adam just nodded his head, without ever allowing his eyes to move from the horrific scene in front of him. The stranger, cleared his throat, "too bad about the smithy huh?" What happened asked Adam? This time, he glanced briefly at the stranger.

Roman Solders, he replied. From what I heard they ran out the occupants and burned the place to the ground. Why? Adam said tears, welling in his eyes, what harm did they ever do to anyone? He said, his voice slightly choking. I am not sure, but I heard that they had to disease of uncleanness, guess they didn't want the whole city getting it, so they burned it all down. Well, he said very non-caring, it was nice meeting you and all but you better move on before one of them solders mistakes you for one of the ones that lived here; they might do more than just run you out of town this time! The stranger's eyes opened wide, you aren't one of them are you? He asked as he backed away slightly from Adam. Saying nothing, Adam just looked at him, turned and walked away, never looking back once. Well! Shalom to you too! Adam heard the stranger bellow as he left. He did not care much about being polite at the moment, I cannot believe how can people be so cruel, he muttered to himself, that place was all Simeon had in this whole world, tears now slowly fall down Adams cheek, he brushes them away, not wanting to give anyone in this place the satisfaction of seeing him upset when all around him are many people going about their business, busy with themselves and their own lives, problems and concerns, it's life as usual in that Great City or is it? Adam looks all around him, and all he sees is a sea of people, going here and there, in and out, buying and selling, is there not one caring person left in this place, he whispers? Lowering his head, Adam sadly turns and leaves thru the huge gates that he came thru so many times before feeling alone and defeated, thinking that not even one person noticed his pain. Teacher, why do your eyes fill with tears? A young student asks his teacher as they sit under an olive tree on a hill. The teacher points towards the city's gates, see that man standing amongst the people? I feel his pain, I am sorry for him. Teacher, another one said, there are many by the gate, how do you know which man? Is he one of us? Why are you sad for him? The teacher smiled, they are all one of us, and he is why I am here. Him and all like him. Adam made his way back into the hills, he had made up his mind not to tell Simeon anything about his home, what was the point anyway, Simeon could never go back so why hurt him. So deep in thought was Adam that he didn't notice the group of people that was there off to the side of the road. Shalom, they said to him, startling him out of his thoughts, shalom he replied trying not to act too obvious as he peered over at all the cheese, grapes, wine and bread that they had laid out before them. Noticing his gaze, a woman of the group asked if he was hungry and if he would care to join them. No thank-you, Adam said, more rudely than he intended, I must be getting back. Are you sure, she asked? There's plenty enough, here sit and have some wine. Adam could not resist as the woman poured him some cool wine and made him a plate of cheese and grapes. Thank-you, as he took the plate of food from her. Assuming she was the servant he asked of her, might I inquire of you, which one of these men is your master, so that I may thank him properly? Then all of a sudden they all looked at each other then, at the women and they all broke out in a loud laughter, causing Adam to just look confused then angry and bellow out "what's so funny". The woman held out her arm, perhaps I should introduce myself, my name is Lydia, and these people are my servants! Embarrassed, Adam could feel his face turning three shades of red but he held out his arm anyway. My father owns a cloth making business, she continued and I am the maker of the purple cloth. Oh, was all Adam could say, although he still could feel his face turning redder, if that was possible! Now, she continued, pretending not to notice, eat and relax. Lydia handed Adam his plate, saying, I told you my name, but you haven't told me yours yet? My apologies, Adam replied, my name is Adam. Again with the red face, Lydia thought. Shalom, Adam, she replied, smiling. Shalom, he answered, smiling and losing one shade of red! As the storm clouds, quickly approached, it cooled off the afternoon, and Adam and Lydia passed it by getting to know each other better. Adam told her all about how he had met Roxanne and Simeon and all that had happened to them. Well, mostly all, all except how Simeon was dying, just that he was old and ill and didn't have much time left, but shared all the stories of Roxanne and their adventures together. Lydia shared with Adam her story of her father's cloths, and how he entrusted her to go the great city with the selling of the cloths every year. She shared that she had done so well that he had given her a small room and her own servants to develop her dream of making the purple cloth. She told him what it was like to be a young woman with a business, how hard it was at first, but that the cloth was so beautiful that it practically sells itself. May I see it, Adam asked? Lydia's eyes lit up, I would be honored, she said as she asked one of the men to get it out of the wagon. When Adam saw the cloth, he could not hold back his admiration, the color was such a deep purple, like nothing he had ever seen before! It's the most beautiful cloth I have ever seen, he said. You really think so, she asked? Oh yes, I have never seen such a color! Simeon would love this Adam thought to himself. Say, Lydia, do you think that I could buy some cloth from you? For Simeon, you know for his burial time. Lydia's eyes filled with tears, Adam you take as much as you need, I would be honored. So he did and when he tried to give her the last of his money, she refused. Your friendship today was a gift that I could never put a price on, go in peace Adam, and take care of your friend. Thank-you, Lydia was all Adam could get out he was so taken with her gift. Lydia, a servant came up and said we had better get going the storm is looking worse. Adam and Lydia looked to the sky, they both agreed, and held out each other's arms to hold. It was wonderful meeting you Lydia, Adam said, I hope our paths cross again someday. As well they will, Lydia replied, I must meet this infamous Roxanne you told me so much about! I loved all those stories! She must be a very special friend to you. The best, Adam replied! And I bet she is getting very anxious waiting for my return, with this storm and all. "Again, thank-you and shalom to all of you" Adam bowed! Because of your kindness, you have restored some of my faith back into brotherly love. Smiling Adam made his way down the winding dirt road, a little lighter, carrying all the items that he had bought in the city to make Simeon a wonderful meal, plus a piece of beautiful purple cloth draped over his shoulder. Tonight will be the most comfortable night for Simeon, that I can possible make it, I owe him that and so much more, he thought to himself, as he walked as fast as he could trying to beat the storm, to his dying friend and his loyal Roxanne. Not wanting the cloth to get wet or ruined Adam stopped long enough to fold the cloth and place it inside his shirt, the same place where he used to keep the blue blanket his mom made him to keep it safe, next to his heart. On he went as fast as his legs would let him to what he thought would be a peaceful night taking care of Simeon and telling them both all about his day and Lydia, as they ate the best meal they all had eaten in a very long while. Little did he know that it would be by far a very, very different kind of night!!

# PART TEN; INTRUDERS

Staring down into the vast land Roxanne sniffs the air, trying to get any familiar scent of her beloved friend Adam, where is he, she wondered as she once again, climes the hill a few feet away from Simeon, looking to see if she can spot Adam, but all that there was in the air was an ever increasing promise of an impending storm. Looking up at the very dark clouds, Roxanne starts pacing back and forth, stops and looks again at the horizon but in the opposite direction. There she sees something! A cloud of dust rising above the ground, could it be, she hopes, sniffing the air again trying to use every instinct she can to feel if her Adam is coming home. She sniffed again, nothing. Confused, Roxanne remembered Adam telling her to keep her eyes on the other dirt road, that soon he would return and she would see him walking up on that road, but that was the opposite road. This dust cloud is on the other dirt road, and it's getting close fast. Roxanne quickly ran back down the hill to check on Simeon, he did not look well at all, but for now he was sleeping peacefully and in no pain. She grabbed the side of his blanket with her teeth, and pulled it up over his shoulder, took one last look around making sure that he would be safe, and started running down the road, opposite of where Adam said to watch and wait. She went running towards something she knew not, friend or enemy. The closer she got, the more she convinced herself that she was running towards her Adam, and then suddenly she came to an abrupt stop! Sniffing the air she got an all too familiar smell, no not the smell of her friend and companion, but one of another animal, and one of sweat. Fear, took over her whole being and overwhelmed Roxanne, these scents are not good, so she hid herself behind a huge rock, there she waited till she could get a good look at what frightened her so. Peering from behind the rock, straining to see, and trying to put faces with the smells, Roxanne's eyes open wide as a small whimper escapes from her throat, just below her and down the road was a group of Roman Solders! They had stopped to water their horses and rest. As quickly as quietly as possible Roxanne headed back towards Simeon and hopefully Adam would also be there by now. As swiftly as she could, Roxanne made her way back, but now the rain had also began, and by the sound of the thunder, and the flash of the lightening, it was not going to be letting up any time soon. So bravely, Roxanne runs, and runs, trying desperately to put the fear she feels welling up, aside, because after all Adam did put her in charge, till he returned. And she wanted him to be proud of her and prove that she could handle the responsibility. By the time she reached Simeon, the rain was no longer just a sprinkle, but a steady pouring out of water and Simeon was getting quiet wet, so Roxanne grabbed the edge of the mat that Adam had woven together and started to pull Simeon towards the mouth of a nearby cave. Simeon's weight had dropped quite a bit so it wasn't too difficult for her to get him there fairly quickly, even though she was tired from her run before. She pulled him far back into the cave where it was dry and away from the rain that had now started to fall very hard and fast, covered him with the blanket, and laid down beside him, listening and waiting. Between the rain, thunder, and Simeon's quiet breathing, Roxanne gave in to her exhaustion and fell into a restless sleep. KABOOM! Yelp- Roxanne's eyes flew open wide as a flash of lighting lit up the cave and the crack of thunder caused Roxanne to jump up and growl, her fur standing up on the back of her neck! Looking around now seeing what she hoped to see, still no Adam, she wined, trying, Roxanne, Simeon weakly opened his eyes, are you here? Roxanne immediately went over to Simeon and places her paw on his arm, there you are girl, and he places his hand on her head to pet her. Thank-you for staying by me girl I know Adam will be back soon, don't worry, and with that he fell back into a deep sleep. Roxanne stayed a few minutes longer, and then went over to the mouth of the cave, it was beginning to be midday, maybe just one more look down the road, she thought, so she braved the rain, and started towards the hill, very mindful of those solders she saw earlier, climbing up the hill she stared down the road, and her eyes light up, she could not see anything, but her nose took in that wonderful, wonderful scent that she knew so well as her Adam, there not too far away . Then she saw him, running thru the mud and puddles as fast as he could, towards the last place they were at, a few feet away from where Roxanne had pulled Simeon out of the rain and into the cave. Roxanne no longer could contain herself; she let out a joyful howl and took off fast, down the hill towards her beloved Adam! Meeting him halfway and jumping into his arms, knocking him over onto the ground, right into a huge mud puddle, but neither one of them cared, they were both so happy to see each other! Roxanne! Adam exclaimed, I sure missed you girl, licking his face all over, Roxanne exclaimed the same sentiment! Not caring that they were covered in mud from head to paw, and for just a moment enjoying the simple moment of being loved and together with a best friend. That moment however, didn't last, just as quick and the joy came, it left with Roxanne remembrance of those solders just down the way and that Simeon was all alone at the cave, not looking so good either. Roxanne grabbed Adam's sleeve and pulled at it, what's the matter, girl he asked as he got to his feet, wondering why she changed her mood so abruptly. Roxanne started running back up the road, and towards the hill, turning around, she grabbed at his hand again and pulled him towards the hill, then once again running up the road and barking, finally convincing Adam to start to run and follow her, thinking that Simeon had taken a turn for the worse. Or that maybe he was too late altogether, to make that wonderful dinner for Simeon that he had planned, praying that he wasn't every step became faster till finally they were going up the hill and almost at the cave. When Adam realized that Roxanne had pulled Simeon into the cave to get him out of this terrible rain, he felt very proud and impressed with her. But to his surprise Roxanne ran past the cave and down the dirt road behind it. Girl wait, where are you going, he yelled? But the wind and rain just carried his words away, afraid she would get lost or hurt he struggled to keep up. When he finally did catch up to her, she was at a complete stop, just standing there, staring down the road, sniffing, what girl he gasped trying to catch his breath, what do you smell? Just then, Adam saw what she was looking at, movement, down the road, just below them, at the bottom of the hill, what he saw sent a chill up his spine, solders and horses!! Adam dropped to his knees! Grabbing Roxanne, he mutters, now what are they doing here? Up to no good I'm sure., let's get back to the cave and to Simeon, Quickly! They barley arrived at the mouth of the cave when Adam heard the pounding of horse hoofs, and a loud voice commanding him to stop! Adam froze, go into the cave girl he whispered to Roxanne, she just looked at him and whimpered. Go on Roxanne, Adam said a little more sternly tend to Simon, go now! Reluctantly, Roxanne turned to the safety of the cave's darkness, back farther but not so far that she couldn't come to Adam's rescue if she needed to. As the solders approached, Adams heart pounder harder and faster, there were about twenty of them as far as he could tell, and in the middle of them was something they were pulling or dragging, he couldn' tell which. The first solder came to a halt just a few inches away from Adam. Turn around slowly, he ordered. Adam did so. State you name, the solder again ordered. My name is Adam. The solder narrowed his eyes and inched his very tall, very skittish horse closer to Adams body leaning over within inches to Adams face, and narrowing his eyes he orders, "State your full name". Adam squares his jaw, that is my full name, far as I can remember, he says with as much calmness as he can muster up. Ahh, the solder straightens back up onto his horse; you're one of those nameless beggars, eh? He snidely remarks. In the darkness of the cave Roxanne, lets out a low warning growl, not liking the treatment her Adam was getting by those other humans. What's that noise! A solder remarks, it came from inside that cave! The leader, got off his horse, and drew out his sword. That, was nothing, Adam said nervously and as loudly as he could, silently upset with Roxanne for making any noise, yet knowing why and proud at the same time. But before he could say anything else or move in the solders way, another solder grabbed him from behind and was holding him. Then suddenly, from somewhere towards the middle of the group of solders, a loud voice cried, "I wouldn't go in there", " Death is in that cave"," Death and sickness!" The solder stopped cold in his tracks. Adam tried to turn around and see just who or where that voice was coming from, but that darn solder's grip was just too tight. How anyone could know about Simeon, or that he was in that cave, he hasn't made any noise. Even I don't know if he's still alive, I haven't been able to see him yet, Adam thought, so how this person knows, enough to say what he said made Adam very baffled. Adam gave the solder holding him a very angry look, in the hopes that he would loosen his tight grip, he did not. Whatever is in there, come out now! Demanded the Captain of the solders! What's in there the captain demanded as he stood at the mouth of the cave peering into the darkness. Adam thought about lying, but he never was any good at it, and if they did go in and find out they would kill him for lying to them. So he did what he thought best, told the truth. In there is just what that voice back there said, Death and Sickness! Adam said. For that remark he got, struck across the face and knocked to the ground, spilling all the contents of the ingredients of the great supper that was slowly becoming less and less able to happen as time went on. Gaining back his composure Adam stood up and looked the Captain squarely in the eyes, my dying friend is in there, he is covered with sores, heard some people call it leprosy, other call it disease of sinners, uncleanliness, but whatever it's called by it kills, not only the one that has it but anyone who is around them to long also. It's also very painful, so that's probably the noise you heard, him screaming in agony, but you go ahead, see for yourself, if you don't believe me. Once again the captain turned to look into the darkness, stepping to go inside, and once again that voice from behind Adam cries even louder "Death is in there! Do not go in!" This caused the captain to stop his entrance into the cave. Unfortunately not for long, he took a small step into the darkness, Roxanne crouching down in front of Simeon, ready to defend him, if need be, not moving watching, she waits. He cautiously makes another small step inside the blackness, sword in hand, eyes squinting, trying to see into the emptiness, using all his training and senses he had the captain took a deep sniff of the stale cave air. Then for some reason, turned quickly and muttered something Adam could not understand and yelled at his next in command, storms let up, get the men in formation, the Emperor is waiting for this prisoner! What about him? The solder holding Adam asked. Adam braced himself for the worse, waiting for the sharp steel blade to cut into him. The captain looked intently at Adam, then said "let him go he's not worth the trouble"! Immediately, the solder's tight grip loosened, and he roughly pushed Adam away causing him to stumble and fall to the ground. Consider yourself lucky, the captain's in a good mood today; he said sarcastically, as he mounted his horse. Adam decided that the ground was a good place to stay till all the solders had ridden away, so he just stayed there, half kneeling half sitting, wanting to find out where the voice was that help him so much from keeping them from discovering Roxanne and Simeon. Move out, the captain yelled!

Slowly the solders, started to leave, moving in front of Adam single file, as they went by Adam could hear chains moving about half way down the line, looking he could barely make out the figure of a man. The closer the figure got Adam could see that he was restrained by those chains, being pulled by a solder in front of him by a chain around his wrists, he had no shoes on and only was wearing a animal hair's clothing of some kind. Suddenly, he was there, right in front of Adam. Adam's eyes flew open wide, he was older, his hair was longer and he had a beard, but there is no mistaking the kindness in the eyes. Adam was sure this was the boy that had saved him and Roxanne, in the desert from that horrible sand storm, all those years ago! Just as Adam was getting ready to open his mouth to say something, anything to try and help this person that saved him so long ago, out of his situation, their eyes met, and as if they had spoken to each other and understood, Adam's mouth closed, the man shook his head no and held a finger to his lips, then with a jerk of his chain, by the solder, suddenly he was gone, leaving Adam all alone, sitting there for a moment frozen, sad, and exhausted, trying, to understand all that just took place. How did he know there was someone in the cave that needed protection? And why didn't he want me to help him? And what did he do to get arrested for anyway? While Adam was lost in his thoughts, Roxanne was running so fast to him, knowing now it was safe, as she jumped square into his arms and gave him a face licking like he never had before, causing him to forget all that he was wondering about before, and focus on what was most important now, his Roxanne and Simeon! Roxanne had never been more happier to see him than she was at that moment, ok, ok girl, he laughed, I missed you too. Then he remembered Simeon, come on Roxie, let's go check on our pal. Quickly they gathered all the things that had spilled onto the ground, when the solders came, including the beautiful purple cloth, which had gotten a little wet and muddy from the rain that had fallen. Come on, let's get inside, before the next storm hits, Adam told Roxanne, who was already heading into the cave. Adam stopped at the mouth, realizing now what caused the captain to turn from the cave. Being away from Simeon, he had forgotten, or was it that much worse? Adam couldn't help but put the purple cloth over his face as he stepped inside, the stench overpowering even thru the cloth. I will get used to it again, but I don't remember it being so strong, slowly his eyes grew used to the darkness as he made his way following Roxanne to the back of the cave, where he hoped to find Simeon there still alive. Simeon, Adam said softly, it's me, I finally made it back. I have some surprises for you! Simeon? Adam feared the worse when he heard nothing back from the blackness, then he heard it, weak as it was, a cough, it was music to Adams ears. He moved a litter faster to his friends, side, dropping the cloth and feeling his way on his hands and knees, finally he felt the sticks of the bed he made for him, Simeon, Adam said softly, trying to get his eyes focused in the dark as he moved closer. . Simeon, he said again as he touched what he thought was his hand, it felt very cold. A very weak raspy voice cut through the darkness, my friend, the voice said, your home! Yes, Adam said, as he felt a great relief lift off his heart. How are you? No answer at first, then a very small unsure," I'm cold" came out of the darkness. Ok, Adam said, I'll make you a fire, to keep you warm, so hold on Simeon, I'll be right back, ok? There was no response from the darkness. With urgency Adam cried; come on Roxanne, let's get some dry wood. As quickly as he could Adam followed the now dimming sunlight wall of the cave to the mouth, searching for any dry wood along the way, with Roxanne picking up what she could and placing it in a pile in the middle of the cave. Slowly, they finally found enough and they dragged it all back to where Simon was, it didn't take long for Adam to get a fire going, he had built many fires in his lifetime of living homeless, that he had become quite an expert at it. As the fire grew and the cave came alive with light and warmth, Adam stood up at held his hands out to warm them, asking Simeon if he could feel the warmth of the fire yet. When he got no response, he turned finally able to see his old friend, letting out a gasp, truing desperately not to look horrified, Adam forced a smile on his lips, and asked again, in as steady a voice as he could say, he asked again, Simeon, are you getting warm now? Simeon looked at Adam, with gratefulness, yes thanks, and then closed the only part of his face that was not yet touched by the leprosy, his eyes, and he fell into a deep sleep. Adam just sat there, tears falling down his face, he could hardly believe this mass of red oozing sores, used to be the face of his dear friend. The nose was mostly gone, eaten away, so were most of his lips. His face was red with sores and most of his fingers were missing, Adam didn't even want to think about what the rest of his body must look like. Looking at his friend now and remembering how he was before, was just too painful for Adam, and so he did the only thing that he could think of doing. He started to make the special stew for him, with the things that he had brought back with him from the city, knowing that this probably was going to be Simeon's last supper Adam wanted it to be his best one ever . The moon was high in the sky and the savory smell of stew filled the cave's warm air. Adam did not realize how hungry he was till the smell of the stew started to make his stomach growl, then realizing that poor Roxanne had not eaten in a while either, he called her name, barley getting it passed his lips, before she was there bowl in mouth, hardly able to contain her excitement at the prospect of eating such a wonderful meal. Laughing, Adam took the bowl from her, and put some stew in it blowing on it to cool it off for her. Hold on now, Adam laughs as he tries to put the bowl onto the ground for her, as she jumps trying to get at it, be careful, Roxanne it might still be a little hot. Even Simeon, now with the warmth of the fire and the smell of the stew, felt well enough to open his eyes and ask for some help so he could be propped up some, "to see that fire's warmth", and" smell that stew's air better" as he put it. Adam moved him up as carefully as he could, but he could tell that he was in awful pain. Is that comfortable enough for you, he asked? Yes, thanks Simeon softly replied, trying not to scream out his pain. Now knowing what else to do Adam busied himself with keeping the stew from burning. Roxanne, feeling less hungry, went over and curled up close to Simeon, laid down and went to sleep. You know Adam, Simeon suddenly spoke, do you remember the day we met? Sure I do, Adam replied. Just like it was yesterday, why?

Well, he asked, do you remember that young fellow, the one that helped you in the street, when Roxanne got ran over by that chariot? Do you mean the young man who came out of nowhere, touched what I thought, no, knew was a dead Roxanne, and said she was just sleeping and brought her back to life, and then took off, or disappeared, before I could even comprehend what had happened? Is it that young man you're asking about? Yes, Simeon said slowly, that young man. Why do you ask, Adam said? Well, I never told you this before, but I had an encounter of sorts with him also. Adam turned quickly from stirring the stew, to face Simeon. You did, he said astonished! Where? Oh, years before I met you. That, young man, well he was just a boy then. I was walking down the dirt road, to get supplies, and as I passed the temple I saw a large crowd looking into the temple, being a curious sort, I went over and entered the outer court area; you know where the women are, on the temple Sabbath. Simeon took a painful breath. If this is too much for you, Adam said, Simeon interrupted him, no I want to continue, just bear with me a moment. Take your time Adam said, with all the compassion that he felt in his heart. Simeon began again, after pushing my way thru the people, to the front; it was there that I first saw him. He was sitting there in front of all these Scribes and Pharisees, and believe it or not it was him that was teaching them! I don't believe it, exclaimed Adam! Are you sure of what you seen? I am just as sure as I am of this pain that is as real to me today. Not only was he teaching them, Simeon continued, they were actually asking him questions, mostly I think to trip him up, but instead they were astonished by his answers! That is a wild story, Adam said imagine that, a simple child teaching the elite learned of God! Hold on, Simeon said as he tried to adjust himself a little higher against the cave wall, I'm not finished yet. So there I was standing there, astonished, with my mouth open, straining trying to hear all that they were talking about, when a very soft voice from behind cried," look there, he is there"! I turned around, and saw a very young, very worried woman and a slightly older man standing behind her looking just as worried, looking to where she was pointing. She was pointing as that child teaching in the temple. So those must have been his parents, Adam said. Well they must have because they called to him and he came out, immediately standing next

40

to them, leaving all those learned priest's, just sitting there scratching their heads and beards and arguing amongst themselves the day's events. Next, thing I knew, I turned to leave and there he was standing there right in front of me. Staring right at me! Simeon stared into the fire; I can still see those eyes. Amazing, aren't they, Adam says! That word doesn't even begin to describe them Simeon replied. It's like they look right through you, right to your very soul. Seemed like it was forever, him looking at me, and me looking into those eyes, then he said what I thought was the strangest thing; at the time anyway. What, Adam cried, now, so interested in this story that he almost forgot all about the stew. Moving over, he stirred it and quickly went back over to Simeon leaning closer to hear, as Simeon was starting to get very weak and tired. He told me that soon I was going to be a blessing to someone, and that I will be put through a great trial, but to be at peace, because God has seen my heart and has touched it with his love. Wow, Adam whistled, how come you never said anything, till now? Well, when we first met, you never told me about that time in the street with the young man. Didn't want you to think I was crazy or anything, Adam replied. Hey, wait a minute Adam stated, how do you know about that time in the road, I never did tell you, and how do you know this child is the same one as the young man in the road? What are you not telling me Simeon? Well, I was actually there, in the crowd that day, watching it all, thought Roxanne was dead too! So I was leaving just as that fellow was kneeling next to you. As I was turning to go he walked right past me, he smiled at me, and he had those same eyes as that boy at the temple. There is only one set of eyes like those, yes I'm sure it was the same person. I could hardly believe it when you came running into the stable, with Roxanne, breathing, alive and all! Any way I probably didn't tell you about the boy for the same reason that you didn't tell me," didn't want you to think me crazy or anything"! Both of them said that at the exact same time, laughing together for the first time in a long time, Adam got up of the cave floor and went over to take the stew off the fire. That was an amazing story Simeon, sure gave me and appetite, how about you? Getting a bowl, Adam put some of the stew into it and blew on it, not hearing Simeon's answer he, he said, I hope you're hungry, Simeon I made this stew just for you! No answer. Simeon? Adam called out again. Getting a very sick feeling in the pit of his stomach and hearing a small cry coming from Roxanne Adam turned, dropping the bowl of stew and rushing to his friend's side, seeing Simeon, who was just sitting there with this half smile on his face, looking up into the cave's darkness. Look Adam, he said trying to point with his fingerless hand, everything will be ok, he's back, I told you I would never forget those beautiful eyes. Looking up Adam stared into the cave's dark heights, wanting to say that he didn't see anything, but instead just saying, it's going to be ok Simeon, just rest now. Then Simeon looks at Adam and says, "I love you Adam, remember you are never alone", then he looks back up into the cave's darkness, smiles again and dies. Suddenly Roxanne lets out a long loud very sad howl, which cuts right through to Adam's soul. Picking up Roxanne, he holds her close, it's ok, sweetheart, he says as he tries to console her, he's not in any more pain now, not believing his own words of comfort he puts her down, his eyes tearing up he gets that beautiful purple cloth and places it over Simeon's body . I love you too Simeon, Adam whispers you were the father that I had lost at such a young age. Adam goes to close Simeon's eyes that were still looking up into the cave's heights, closing his eyes he gently places the cloth over his face. Picking up Roxanne, and the shovel he walks out into the darkness, hurting so badly he could barely see out of the tears that were falling freely down his face, Adam went looking for a special place where he could bury his dear friend, coming upon the place, where he buried Roxanne's mother at he decided to bury him there next to her. Sadly, Adam begins the task of digging the final resting place for his last human friend on the face of this earth, or so he thinks!

# PART ELEVEN; LOST AND CONFUSED

H e just sat there; numb staring out into nothingness, for seemed like an eternity. Now that his reasons for all that he did each day, all the things that kept him going, his purpose so to speak, his responsibilities to Simeon and all his care, had died with him, Adam wasn't quite sure what to do next, or even if he felt like doing anything. After he carefully and lovingly wrapped Simeon in the beautiful purple cloth, he and Roxanne put Simeon on the homemade mat and pulled him over to where Roxanne's mother was buried. There Adam laid Simeon to rest, next to her, and he made a star of David over the mound and a small sign that simply read; "Here lies Simeon, closest person to a father I had and best friend ever to me and Roxanne. Then Adam sat down on the ground, put Roxanne onto his lap, and hasn't moved since. The sun was high in the sky by then; with dark clouds looming a threat of another storm was imminent. Roxanne, feeling her Adam's pain, didn't move much herself, she slept some, waking now and then to look at her master, checking to see if he was still there somewhere inside, behind those eyes she's come to know and read so well. It was now becoming dusk, and the wind was beginning to become quite insistent on trying to get Adam's attention. Still numb, and in his own pain, Adam was oblivious to the cool wind or anything else around him, until Roxanne still lying in his lap, started shivering. That little movement alone from, his Roxanne was enough to bring Adam back to her. Now there, he said quietly as he picked her up from his lap and held her close to his heart, don't be afraid, I will keep you warm he told her, as he himself started getting up, I will take care of you always. Let's go back to the cave, and try and figure out what we're going to do with the rest of our lives, ok girl? So, not knowing what else to do back to the cave they went, fighting the ever increasing wind along the path, to the only home they had. By the time they arrived, the sun was setting and darkness was overtaking the land. Adam stopped at the mouth of the cave, remembering, looking at Roxanne he said, "This is going to be harder than I thought girl". Then suddenly it started to rain, and a loud crack of thunder caused Roxanne to let out a yelp, and run inside to the safety of the cave. Ok, ok Adam said, I'm right behind you! Stepping inside the cave's darkness, he could barely make out the place where Simeon had been laying; the fire had died down, with the pot of stew still sitting there right where Adam had left it cold and ruined. Adam shivered, not so much from the cold, as from the coldness of a place that just a few days ago seemed alive with warmth and yes a home. Maybe, if I get a fire going again, he thought; even salvage some of the stew? Roxanne's must be hungry; perhaps if I do that this cave will be like it was before. So that's what he did. Sitting now by the fire's warmth, watching Roxanne enjoy what little stew he could salvage, himself eating some bread and a cool drink of spring water, Adam's spirits lifted slightly. Looking at Roxanne, he smiled, I am so grateful to have you girl, do you understand how much you mean to me? Looking up from her food, with her mouth full Roxanne lets out a bark, her nose full of brown gravy, Adam couldn't help but laugh out loud, long and hard until that laughter suddenly turned into tears, finally allowing Adam to let out all the pain he was keeping inside. Never, since his parents died, did Adam cry so hard and deep. Hearing his anguish, Roxanne immediately leaves her food and goes to his side; she puts her paw on his leg. Picking her up Adam holds her close and mourns for the loss he now has to face. Thankfully, with his Roxanne there he doesn't have to do it alone. Hello? Hello the voice said louder! The sound echoed back to where Adam and Roxanne were sleeping, just out of the firelight, towards the back of the cave. Causing Adam to wake with a start, and Roxanne growling lowly, the voice echoed again, hello, anyone in here? I'm no threat, just wondering if I could get dry and warm by your fire. Adam bolted upright, grabbing the shovel; he used to bury Simeon with earlier. Slowly and as quietly as possible, he inched his way towards the mouth of the cave, and the faceless voice. Roxanne of course was quietly and quickly inching her way towards the back of the cave and behind a rock! The voice rang out again, I mean no harm, I saw your fire from afar off, it's wet, and I'm cold, thought maybe I could just dry off, hello, anyone there? I can hear, you breathing, the voice said, flatly. Adam, rolled his eyes, "step into the light" he said as menacing and threating as he could. The voice stepped into the light and became a man, not to tall, and very wet. He seemed to look nice enough though, so Adam loosened his grip some on the shovel and stepped himself into the light of the fire. Roxanne chose to stay hidden, closer but still hidden behind another boulder, but still giving her threating growl, just in case Adam needed any back up help! What are you doing out here in the hills in the middle of a storm, Adam asked the stranger? I was on my way to the city, to meet someone, and I got caught in this rain storm. Adam just stood there not moving. Honest brother, I do not mean you nor your little pet lamb back there any harm. Looking dumfounded for a moment, Adam blinked at first, and then smiled, then dropping the shovel he was holding as a weapon, he broke out in uncontrolled laughter, and he laughed and laughed and laughed, finally he managed to say as he wiped the tears from his eyes, "my what?" Still not sure what was so funny, the stranger pointed to the rear of the cave, where Roxanne happened to be hiding and still expressing her distaste of this person, your lamb he said, back there making all that noise, is it sick or something? Hearing him ask that only caused Adam to laugh louder and harder! Did I say something amusing? The stranger asked as he crossed his arms over his chest, quickly getting very annoyed at the whole situation. No, No Adam said, I'm sorry, trying to regain his composure. Let me call my uh lamb, maybe that will explain my behavior better. "Roxanne, come here" Adam called out, but nothing happened. "It's ok girl, it's safe, come here", still nothing. Adam cleared his throat, excuse me a moment I'll just go and get her. As the stranger stood there he could hear, "come on Roxanne, oh don't be mad, I didn't mean to laugh, now don't embarrass me come on!" Again the stranger hears more of that strange lamb noise, and then finally out of the shadows comes Adam followed slowly by one very displeased Roxanne! OH! It's a dog, sure did fool me he chuckled as he scratched his forehead. It sure sounded like a little lamb bleating to me. With that comment, Roxanne stuck her nose into the air, snorted, turned around and proceeded to go back to her bowl of food that was on the ground, all the while keeping a watchful, disapproving eye on that stranger. Oh my she sure is a sensitive one isn't she, he asked? I suppose so Adam said, but she'll get over it in her own good time. Neither of us is used to that much company, if you know what I mean. Adam realized that the man was still standing at the mouth of the cave, wet and now starting to shiver a little, I apologize Adam said, come inside and get warm by the fire. The man did so without having to be asked twice. Adam held out his arm, my name is Adam; I have some hot stew, if you're hungry. Yes, thank you, my name is Thomas, the man replied as he shook Adams arm. With that the two sat down by the fire, Adam lost in his own thoughts, Thomas finishing his stew, so grateful to be somewhere warm and dry. This stew is very good, Thomas said breaking the morbid silence. Thanks, was all Adam could bring himself to say, he just didn't have the emotion or strength left in him to explain the past week. Where the stew came from, why he made it, and of course Simeon, and so on, so he decided to turn the conversation and subject off of himself and onto Thomas. So, Thomas he started, you say you're going into the city to meet someone? Who? A relative or perhaps a friend? Just then Roxanne finished her meal came out of the shadows and lay down beside Thomas, allowing him to pet her head. See, Adam said," in her own good time!" Well, hello there girl, I guess she's forgiven me for calling her a lamb. Guess so, Adam said with a smile. She sure is a cutie, Thomas said as he petted her head, well look at that he exclaimed, she has the shape of a heart right on top of her head! I've never seen anything like that before, he said very impressed. Yes, Adam said, it makes her very easy to spot form any other dog, not that I wouldn't know my best friend eh Roxanne! With that Roxanne jumped up and barked the leaped into Adam's arms, giving his face a very sloppy washing with his face! Ok, ok I love you too, Adam said laughing. You and that dog are very close aren't you, Thomas asked? Well, Adam said we have been thru a lot together, and I expect we still have some stuff to get through yet. Anyway, Adam changed the subject not wanting to think of the past anymore, to get back to the question I asked you earlier. Do you have someone special in the city you need to see? I've been there a few times, used to work at a business there; perhaps I know who it is you are going to visit. What's this person's name? Well, I'm not really sure Thomas said. I haven't really met him yet. Oh, Adam said, scratching Roxanne's head. Is he a friend of a friend? No, was all Thomas said. A distant cousin perhaps, Adam asked? I don't think so, replied Thomas. Ok, Adam said very slowly, with a puzzled look on his face. If you don't mind me saying so, you are sure acting very mysterious about this person, or maybe I am prying too much, if so I apologize. Oh no you're not, I'm sorry Thomas exclaimed, putting his head into the palm of his hand. I don't mean to sound so vague; Thomas stared into the fire for a moment before he began to speak again. Finally, he spoke" I know this sounds a little crazy, but this person I'm going to see, I have in never met, to tell you the truth, I really don't even know if he exists! What! Adam exclaimed, now more interested than ever! Tell me more, he said as he motioned with his hand. You're going to think I'm a crazy man, Thomas said. Listen, Adam said as he leaned a little closer to the fire, after what I've been through and the things I've seen, nothing surprises me any more so don't worry, I try not to judge, and I won't think you're crazy, so continue, you have me very intrigued now, and start from the beginning ! Well, Thomas said, there's not a whole lot to say, one day I was just living an ordinary life, minding my own business, taking care of my family. So you have a family, Adam interrupted? Yes, I live with my mother, father, sister and twin brother. Oh, I have heard of twins before, Adam said, but I've never met one before. So tell me Thomas, it must be great to have such a close person that looks just like you to grow up with. Yes, I guess so, Thomas said. But I doubt if anyone would understand how I feel, always having to be one of two alike, never feeling unique. True, Adam added, but knowing that there's another person out there that understands you?

Well, I think that must be something else! I suppose so, Thomas answered, not very convincingly. Somehow Adam got the feeling that he better change the subject back to the original conversation, so he cleared his throat, and replied, "Anyway, back to why you are here meeting this non-existent person". Oh yes, where was I Thomas replied, I remember, It was an especially cool and rainy day so we all finished our chores early. I was especially tired that night so I went to bed early. I fell asleep very fast and deep. Then all of a sudden I had a vision, or maybe a dream I'm not sure which. A vision, Adam asked? Thomas shook his head. Really, Adam said trying not to sound to skeptical, of what? Well, of a man. A man? Yes, a man, with his arms outstretched, and he was speaking. What was he saying, Adam asked? Thomas just stared into the fire for the longest time, the he answered softly, I don't know, I couldn't tell. Adam took a deep breath in, and then let it out. And that's the reason you left your home and family, risked your life and traveled all this way? Because of a dream or supposed vision of a man you have never seen, saying something you couldn't hear? See, Thomas said trying to curb his anger; I knew you would think me crazy, like all of my family did when I tried to explain it to them. I don't think you're crazy, Thomas, Adam said. Ok maybe a little impetuous. What makes you think he is in this particular city? It is just something that I know, Thomas said. I doubt that you would understand. It's still so clear to me, if you could just see his face like I did, to look into those eyes, they still burn in my mind and heart, and I just have to know for sure! Say no more, Adam Interrupted, holding up his hand, burning incredible eyes, that I understand and I really hope you find what or who you are looking for. Thomas took a cleansing breath, thanks he said. I doubt that much will come from all this, but something inside of me is pushing me ahead, so I go. Well, Adam said as he stood up and stretched, go tomorrow, when it's light outside; you are welcome to sleep here tonight. Thanks, I am really quiet tired, so I will take you up on that offer. Shalom, Adam; Thomas said as he lay down to sleep. Sleep well my friend, Adam replied. As Adam laid there that night, he thought about Thomas and his dream, wondering if the same man in his dream could possibly be the same young man Adam had met and the same one that Simeon had met. Seem Like the description of those incredible eyes and kind face, no matter what age is always the same. I wonder, could it all mean something important, something special which ties us all together? Maybe, just maybe, there is something more to life than pain and loss. Then, Simeon's swollen puss infected face came into his mind, as well as the still fresh hurt of it all, and again Adam's heart hardened. No he told himself, there is nothing more, life has taught me that. Right at that moment Roxanne crawled next to him and laid her head on his shoulder. You, however Roxanne are real, and I love you; I cannot afford to believe in a fantasy vision from someone who doubts it himself! With that Adam covered Roxanne with his blanket and fell asleep, satisfied that he had answered the questions in his mind. Morning came too soon for both Adam and Roxanne, but as the sun tapped her warm fingers of light upon Adams back and light filled the mouth of the cave where Adam and Roxanne were sleeping, they couldn't help but open their eyes and face the new day. As Adam started to get up, the first thing he saw was Thomas, kneeling by the fire, smiling and cooking. Good morning, shalom he said, Coffee? All Adam could do was muster up half a smile mutter morning and take the cup of coffee that Thomas was holding out for him. Thanks, replied Adam, Still puzzled as to where this coffee and eggs had come from. After half of that warm coffee had reached his system Adam couldn't help but smile, just as he opened his mouth to ask how all this came about, Thomas started to explain. What! Thomas Said looking innocently over his cup of coffee at Adam. Ok, Ok, I had the stuff in my bag, and I found a wild duck's nest down the way with some eggs in it. Thought I should do something to repay you for all your kindness before I leave. Oh, was all Adam said, then "Thanks". Roxanne, on the other hand was beside herself with hunger. What's she doing, Thomas asked pointing to Roxanne. Is she ok? What, Adam turned quickly to observe Roxanne on her back and all four paws were sticking straight up in the air, her head was off to one side, tongue hanging out the side of her mouth and eye looking straight ahead! Oh, that, Adam said casually, she does that to dramatize the fact that I haven't fed her yet, and she is starving to death! No kidding, said Thomas, trying not to sound too impressed. You sure do have yourself a pretty smart dog there Adam. Sometimes, she's too smart for her own good, Adam replied smiling! You would not believe some of the situations she has gotten herself into. I can't even begin to imagine, replied Thomas as he put a dish of food in front of Roxanne, who immediately came back to life, turned over, barked and started to devour the food. They both started to laugh, yes she sure is something, Adam said she's also my best friend. After they all ate and cleaned up, Thomas packed up and got ready to leave. Well, I'm off to chase my dream, or vision or something, he said as he scratched his head smiling. Shalom, Adam and thanks again. Good luck Thomas, Adam replied as he held out his arm, and I hope you find what or whoever it is you are looking for. Well, I doubt I will, but who knows, Thomas replied, Maybe I will see proof of what I dream of. You can't doubt forever Thomas, there comes a time when you just have to believe, proof or not, Adam said as he put his hand on Thomas's shoulder, and wondering to himself, just where that piece of wisdom came from. I'll try and remember that, Thomas answered as he bent down to say good-by to Roxanne. Taking her paw into his hand he said, now Roxanne, you'll take care of him won't you? She just licked his face and whimpered. Then down the road he went whistling, once again leaving Adam and Roxanne alone. Well girl, I guess it's time for us to decide what were gonna do with the rest of our lives. Little did either of them realize the great trial that lay ahead of them as they both turned and went back inside the cave, not quite knowing what to do next?

# PART TWELVE; ON THE MOVE AGAIN

S itting there staring into the glowing embers with Roxanne, looking lovingly into his face, Adam wanted to stay there in that cave and hide forever. There in the cool darkness, not having to talk to anyone or face any more pain. Looking at Adam's face, so tired and sad Roxanne saw the same hurt that was there in her own eyes when her mother went away, and now Simeon is out there, in the dirt like her mommy. Not understanding all of this, Roxanne, feared the same would happen to her or worse yet to Adam. What would happen to me? Who would take care of me? Suddenly Roxanne became very frightened, and let out a very long very sad cry, as she leaped onto Adams lap, bringing him out of his morbid silence. Crying all the while she climbed up his chest trying to get some sort of solace to be as close to her master as she could. There, now what's the matter Roxanne, what frightened you? Adam held her close to his heart, trying to comfort her. Its ok girl, nothing is going to harm you, I promise. Then she looked at him with eyes that spoke volumes to him. I know, he said, I miss him too, and I'm sorry that he's gone, I did all I could, it just wasn't enough. Come on girl let's get things packed; it's time to move on. After gathering all their stuff, Adam decided to leave the bed that he had made for Simeon right there in the cave, along with a few other things they no longer had need of. Only once did they turn around to take a look at the mouth of the cave, and say good-bye to all the ghosts that they we're leaving behind. With now idea of where to go or what to do Adam found himself walking down the dirt road, towards the only other human being that he felt pulled towards. Someone he thought he would never see again but now needed to see very much. Come on Roxanne, there's a very special lady I want you to meet, her name is Lydia. The moon was high in the sky when they arrived in the small town where Lydia told Adam her and her parents lived. She had said that the cloth workshop was in front of and that her parents had a small house in the back, so Adam figured it shouldn't be too hard to find. I he could only find a place that was opened this late that is, he could ask someone. What is that wonderful smell? Lifting her nose higher, Roxanne tried to sniff the cool night air, taking in the sweet aroma fully, she let out a whimper, causing Adam to stop his march like walk and turn his attention toward her. Seeing Roxanne sitting there, on the side of the dirt road, with her little nose high in the air sniffing, looking so sad and tired, he finally realized just how hard he had pushed her to get this far. Never thinking about stopping or resting or even getting something for her to eat, and knowing that she would follow him till she dropped, which from the looks of her she almost did. Walking over towards Roxanne, he scoops her up in his arms, holding her close I'm so sorry girl, he says softly, I know it's been a long, long day. I promise as soon as I find out where Lydia's parents' house is at well rest, and get you some food ok? Is that a deal? Roxanne, happy to be carried, warm in Adam's arms, gave him a very big kiss right on the top of his nose and rested her head in on his shoulder. Thanks girl, you are my best friend, you know that? Look over there I see a light, so that's where he headed towards, Roxanne well safe and comfy in Adam's arms, fell fast asleep forgetting how hungry she was and letting her exhaustion of all that has happened the past few days win. Drifting deeper, and deeper into sweet nothingness, Roxanne was totally at peace until she felt something cold and wet on her face, bringing her back from her sleep, opening her eyes slowly she gave a loud yelp, startled back to the present, Roxanne eyes flew open wide to see something wet in her face sniffing and grunting right there so close she could see two holes on its ugly face snorting at her! Crying and yelping she backed up, only to knock over a metal cart full of trash, which frightened her even more; it was then that she saw Adam up by the light of a house, and heard him calling for her! Running full speed she heads towards Adam, but is blocked by that awful huge pink thing again! Yip, Yip, Yip she cries loudly, turning Adam sees Roxanne backing up and crying loudly, because she is being blocked by a very large very curious pig! "Oh my", say the lady that Adam has been talking to at the doorway. I hope that mean old stray dog doesn't hurt my precious baby! Come here Sugar, she starts shouting loudly, Sugar come here now; come here before that mean old dog hurts you! Suddenly Roxanne looks up and then looks all around. Did she say there's a mean dog around? Slowly she gets out from under the wood box she was hiding under and looked all around; well I don't see any mean dog around, as she sniffed the air. All I see is that big ugly thing over there by that human lady. I certainly don't see or smell any dog! "Go away mean doggy", leave my Sugar alone! Again Roxanne looked all over and sees nothing, so she slowly and cautiously starts to walk towards Adam, then something flies past her face and she hears that voice again, only louder this time. You, Get out of here! Stopping Roxanne looks around again. No mean dog around, then it hits her, wait, does this human think I'm a mean dog?! Me, sweet little me? Spotting Adam, Roxanne starts running towards him as he starts calling her. Then; nothing but darkness. I am so sorry, the woman kept saying over and over. I had no idea she was yours. Please tell me if you need anything, anything at all ok. You stay here as long as you need too. She shook her head and clicked her tongue, I'm so sorry she cried again, wringing her hands on her dress, with tears in her eyes as she turned to close the door to the guest room. Thank-you replied Adam, were fine, just tired. Finally alone Adam turned his attention to Roxanne laying on a little bed, a small bandage around her head to keep the wound clean. The rock just missed her right eye and caused a cut just above it, knocking her out cold. Gently Adam lifts Roxanne's limp body closer to the pillow on the bed and lays down beside her wrapping the blanket around them, he tried to sleep, thinking about the turn of events this evening. He thought the light in the distance would give him a sense of where he could go to find Lydia's house, never did he think he would be in a strange bed in a strange house, with strangers, holding close his best friend, and praying that this awful wound would not keep her from waking up or being the same Roxanne he loves. Suddenly, all the past few days finally caught up within him and the tears began to fall, slowly at first the fast and hard, like they had their own mind, and all Adam could do was let them fall. So he did, holding Roxanne close he lay there in the dark, allowing all the pain of his heart to surface and melt into tears, finally with the pain spent, he fell into a restless sleep, with dawn only a few hours away. MMM, that is a wonderful smell, I guess it's time to eat, Roxanne sniffed as she opened her eyes wide and moved her head, suddenly causing her head to hurt she gave out a loud yelp. She didn't know what was worse, the pain in her head or that same huge ugly pink thing sniffing her face when she opened her eyes! Before she could react any more Adam was in-between her and that thing and that lady who called her a mean doggy was also there pulling that other thing away, Roxanne tried to growl but she just didn't have it in her. Quickly, Adam picked her up, and started giving her kisses all over her face, Roxanne, your awake, I am so glad you are ok. Roxanne kept one eye on that thing, in the room and tried to give Adam a lick, not sure why she felt so tired, or why her head hurt so. Adam, the lady said, why don't you bring your baby to the kitchen, so I can fix her something to eat. She has to be starving, put her down and see if she can walk. No, Adam said more harshly than he intended, no, he repeated a little softer this time, I think I'll carry her for now. So down to the kitchen they went, a man, his dog, a heavy set elderly lady, and her pet pig! Breakfast was almost done and Roxanne was appearing to feel better, so Adam decided he would try and see if he could find out where Lydia's house was from here. Thank-you for all your help, Adam said, and for allowing us to stay the night. Oh don't even thank me, the lady replied, I still feel horrible for throwing that rock at your sweet little dog. It's just that there are so many wild animals around here and my sugar is so friendly, she thinks all animals and people for that matter are friendly and like her. Yea, how is it that you own a pig? Adam asked. I mean, if you don't mind me asking. Well, first let me introduce myself, my name is Sephria, and I am a Roman citizen. Hello, my name is Adam, I apologize, I should have introduced myself last night but I was so worried about my dog. No problem, Sephria replied I would have done the same thing; her name is Roxanne, correct? Yes, Adam replied, I have taken care of her since she was very small. She has been there for me and I for her through a lot, especially lately. Anyway Adam continued, I know what it feels like to love an animal with all your being. But I must say, never thought in this area of the world would I find someone so devoted to an animal such as Sugar! Oh yes, believe me I know what people here say about pigs, their unclean, dirty, and all, they also treat me the same way, because of my love for Sugar. But as I said before, I am a Roman citizen, and I really don't care what the locals say or how they treat me. Sugar's not a pig to me, she's not unclean, or evil, she's my friend, my family and I love her. Now sit and eat, here give that little pal of yours some food; she has been very patient sitting there with that bandage on her head looking so sad and hungry! At that he smiled, Roxanne turned her attention to Adam, her head now feeling a little better and the smell of the food making her drool out the sides of her mouth. Finally, Adam put the bowl in front of her now go slow girl and take your time he told her not knowing what that head wound did to the inside of her body. Roxanne just looked up, gave a small approving bark, and then proceeded to gobble up all the food as fast as her mouth would allow her to do. Adam just shook his head and looked at Sephria and she laughed saying, perhaps she's related to Sugar after all! And Roxanne, well she didn't move her nose one inch out of that food bowel, not even to see what was so funny! After they had laughed all they could, Adam asked," tell me Sephria, have you ever heard of a cloth making business around here anywhere"? I'm looking for a young woman, who makes purple cloth. Oh yes, you must mean Lydia and her parents! Yes! Adam replied, as he sat up now in his chair, finally he thought I can finally get to where I must go. Do you know where the house is located? I believe; it's a few miles into town she stated. It's located right about in the middle of town- good location for a cloth shop, she added for no reason in particular. Do you know the family, Adam asked? Me? No, replied Sephria, not too many folks to friendly with a lady who's best friend is a pig; if you know what I mean. I did however meet Lydia, sweet girl. I had lost my favorite sheep, (another pet I had) Sephria said as she smiled and petted sugar's ears, anyway she had died of old age, poor old gal and Lydia happened to be going by, she was coming back from the city trying to sell some of her parents cloth during their Passover feast a few years back. Well I was very upset, sitting on the ground, holding Lambkins,(that was her name you know she told Adam), as I sat there crying hysterically, I look up and see this sweet young lady in front of me, she asked me if I was ok, and if I needed any help. I was so upset I couldn't even speak. Then she did something so kind I will never forget it. She went and got a shovel, and all alone dug a grave for my precious Lambkins, buried her, even said a little prayer. Then she stayed with me awhile. She even gave me a piece of that beautiful purple cloth she makes so I could wrap Lambkins in it before she placed her in the grave. Sweet girl that one, never once did she care about Sugar, or say that we were unclean or dirty. Still stops in now and then when she travels to the city, just to check in on me and Sugar. Well, Adam said, I am an old friend of hers; do you suppose you could point me down the right road to her parent's place, after I help clean up? I think Roxanne is well enough to travel after that display of eating frenzy, and besides, it's time to move on, we have imposed long enough on your kindness. Well, Sephria replied; first of all your two are always welcome in our house, and second, you're a guest, I won't have you cleaning up anything. Now go upstairs and gather your things and I will show you the right road to take into the town where Lydia's house is at. Standing on her porch Adam gave Sephria a big hug, "thank-you for all you've done for me and Roxanne". Sephria picks up Roxanne, and gave her a big hug, "now Roxanne no more barking at my precious anymore, ok", and gave her a kiss on her nose. Roxanne barks and licks her face. Then out of nowhere, that big pink thing, with the big nose comes barreling out of the house and stands right next to where Sephria is getting ready to put her down, she yelps and leaps out of Sephria's arms and into Adam's practically knocking both of them over in the process. I guess she will never get used to Sugar, Adam says with a sigh! With that he picked up their belongings, turned once again to say thank-you and started down the road, off again towards Lydia, this time closer than ever now.

# PART THIRTEEN; LEARNING TO LOVE

He had finally arrived! Now that he was standing at her front door, he was having second thoughts; what am I doing here, he thought, she barley knows me, I barley know her! Her family is going to think I am crazy! Traveling all this way to tell a woman I hardly know that someone she never met is dead! Adam you are a fool! He said out loud to himself. What were you thinking? Just as he was turning to walk away, the door flew opened, and there she was! She was just as pretty as he remembered, and him standing there, all his belongings in one arm, holding, Roxanne, fidgeting in the other, and with a dumb look on face! She just stares at them for a moment, then her large dark eyes flew open wide with recognition! Adam, she cried, is it really you! Wrapping her arms around his neck giving him a hug, shocked that she remembered him, Adam almost dropped Roxanne. Only by her growling at her disapproval of this human female person hugging her master, did Adam remember that he was holding Roxanne. What a surprise, Lydia continued, what are you doing here? Just then, a very large, very loud man comes to the door bellowing "Lydia, who is this stranger you are so graciously hugging on my porch"?! Roxanne, who is now on the ground, changes her growling to whimpering, and hides herself behind Adam's legs. Peeking just slightly, letting her curiosity overcome her fear of this large human and his very loud voice! Oh papa stop, Lydia says calmly, this is my friend Adam, I told you about him, remember? I met him outside the city when I went there this last time to sell my cloth. Adam, she said turning to the man; this is my father, Petros. Shalom, Adam said nervously, as he held out his arm. Shalom, said, Petros not letting his eye stray from Adam's as though he was trying to read he's very soul through his eyes. And this cutie must be the famous Roxanne, Lydia said trying to break the ice. Yes, this is said Adam, grateful for the change of direction of conversation, but as he tried to step aside, so they could see Roxanne, she would move so she would stay right behind his legs. Strange replied Adam, usually she is very friendly. Why does she have a bandage on her head, Lydia asked? Well, we had a little mishap with the lady at the edge of town and her umm pet, Adam answered. Say no more, Lydia said as she raised her hand, Sugar and Sephria, right? Yes, said Adam with a smile. Is Roxanne ok, asked Lydia? Oh, she'll be fine; I guess she is just a little shy right now. Lydia, a voice sounded out delicately, from inside the house. Where are your manners! Why don't you invite the gentleman in! Oh yes, I'm sorry Adam, come in and meet my mother. Bring Roxanne with you; our house is your house. Thank-you Adam replied, as he entered the house, having to carry Roxanne of course, being she wasn't about to enter it on her own. Trying to maneuver his way around Lydia's father and his glaring eyes proved to be a little more intimidating than Adam had expected. Finally inside, he sees a petite woman standing by the fire, next to an equally as petite chair, holding out her hand. Shalom, I'm Rebecca, Lydia's mother, the woman said. Standing in front of her Adam holds out his arm, expecting Rebecca to grab it, but she just stands there, holding out her arm way below his. Lydia whispers into his ear "she's blind, Adam, you need to bend down and take her hand". His face instantly red Adam quickly and gently takes Rebecca's hand and arm into his and says "shalom", it's very nice to meet you. My, Rebecca replies I can tell that from the sound of your voice that you must be very handsome! Mother, Lydia interrupts, her face turning red! "May I touch your face", Rebecca asks Adam, totally ignoring her daughters embarrassment. Adam looks at Lydia with a questioning look, touch my face? It's how she sees Adam, if she can feel something; she can get a picture of it in her mind. Amazing, replied Adam! Umm yes, ma'am, I would be honored. So Rebecca started to reach her arms up, and Adam bent down towards her hands till his face and her fingers met. Suddenly Roxanne starts this low menacing growl just as Rebecca was getting started to feeling his face, causing her to pull her hands back startled, Oh my, what was that! That, Adam replied as he gave Roxanne a very stern look, I'm sorry to say, is my usually very friendly dog Roxanne, who at the moment is not being very nice! Here, said Lydia, let me hold her, animals love me! As Lydia reached for Roxanne that same low growl came out of her accompanied with some very white, very sharp teeth showing also! Which causes Lydia to back up also; well I guess my way with animals it not that great after all! Smiling slightly, "oh give her to me" Lydia's dad said as he made his way across the room. Come on Roxanne, we'll go into the kitchen and see if I can find you some food. Well, food was all Roxanne needed to hear, she barked and wagged her tail, practically leaping into Petros arms, surprising everyone, even Lydia's father! Well, he said I guess I have the way with animals today, eh Lydia? Lydia just gave him one of those looks, so he turned back to Adam clearing his throat, mind if I take her to the kitchen he said to the point. No, Adam said, and thank-you sir for helping with her. I don't understand what has gotten into her, she is usually so friendly. Seems to me that she has a problem with the females of this house, replied Petros, as he turned and headed towards the kitchen again with a slight smile on his face, and Roxanne in his arms! For a moment no one said a word, and then Rebecca softly spoke, Adam, still up to letting me get a picture of your face in my mind? Of course, Adam said, as he again bent down closer so Rebecca can touch his face, her own face with a look of deep concentration upon it. As she traveled her fingers over his forehead, eyes, nose and lips, each time stopping momentarily as if to let the picture form more details in her mind. Finally she places her arms by her side. You know Adam she says smiling, I was right; you are a very handsome man! With that comment, Adam didn't know what to say except, thank-you. But, she continues, I feel much pain also; I suspect that if I could actually look into your eyes, I would see a lot of sorrow in them. Now Adam was really uncomfortable, how she can tell this, just by touching my face he wondered, but before he had or could respond Lydia came to the rescue. Come on Adam, she took his arm; let me show you the rest of the place, and the workshop before it gets too late. Lydia directs him towards the door, mother we'll be back soon, she says as they leave. Very nice to meet you Adam, Rebecca says. You also, replied Adam. May we talk later Rebecca asks Adam? Sure, I would like that, he says as Lydia whisks him out the door and towards the cloth work shop. Sorry about all that, Lydia says, my mother prides herself on "seeing", thru to people's soul, even though see can't physically see, if you know what I mean. Its ok, Adam said, she was more right than wrong, as you also know! Roxanne kept a listening ear as she ate her food, closely listening to Adam and those two other female humans! She did not like their scent, or the way they touched her Adam so much! And why did he get such a goofy look on his face when that Lydia human is near him? She is one I will a keep close watch on Roxanne thought as she finished her meal and Petros let her out onto the front porch to let her food settle. So, Mr. Adam, Lydia says, what really brings you way out here anyway, besides my charming self! Smiling slightly, he got silent for a moment, not sure if it was the right time to say anything about Simeon or not. Might as well get it over with, he thought. Lydia looked at him, something's wrong, isn't it? Your eyes are full of sadness, come here, let's sit down on this bench, under my favorite tree, we can see the shop later. As they sat down, the sun was starting to get low in the sky, and it was getting to be late afternoon, and the air was cooling down. Lydia shivered, but it was not because of the weather, she took his hand into her own and looked deep into his eyes, tell me she said. Adam had never felt comfortable talking to someone about his deep feelings, especially anyone of the female type, except for Roxanne of course. But Lydia, she was different; he felt totally comfortable with her, but he still hesitated, the pain of Simeon's death still very raw. Adam, do you feel that someone else to talk to would be better? I mean, she said, someone that you would feel more comfortable with? My mother perhaps? No, Adam said. How about my father? Oh no, Adam said a little too quickly, I mean you're not the problem he said quickly! Oh, she said, you know you don't have to say anything; we can just sit here awhile. No, I came here to let you know something; I just didn't realize how hard it would be to actually say the words. Well, she added, why don't you just start at the beginning and see where it leads. Ok, Adam said as he took a deep breath in. Do you remember that beautiful purple cloth that I got from you? Yes, she said. Do you remember what I told you why I wanted it for? Well, let me think, you told so many wonderful stories that day, mostly about Roxanne and your adventure's, and you told me about your friend Simeon, how he was ill, and that you wanted to use the cloth for a bur...., Oh Adam, he died, didn't he? Is that what you have been wanting to tell me? Yes, was all Adam could say as he looked down at the ground, at all the fallen leaves, trying to focus on the red and silver colors of them instead of looking at her face, afraid if he did he would not be able to handle what he saw there in her eyes. Oh Adam I'm so sorry, Lydia said as she gave him a hug, he welcomed the comfort, I feel as though I got to know him well through all of your stories. Was it sudden? I know you said he was ill, and that you were using the cloth to bury him in. I guess I just didn't realize that it would be this soon. Adam stayed silent, afraid to say anything, the loss still to fresh to his heart. Roxanne sat up, there across the way was her Adam and that human, she gave a low growl, and just then Petros came to the porch to sit with her. Well, Roxanne, I know just how you feel, he said, I'm not too sure about your master with my girl. I saw how she looked at him when you two first arrived, and it worries me! I realize that most girls Lydia's age are already married and that your master is a bit older than her, but to me she will always be my little girl, so I also will be keeping a close eye on those two also. Looking up at Petros, Roxanne gave an agreeable bark! For now I guess I just have to trust in them both, eh Roxanne? Guess I'll go in and see if Rebecca needs anything, Petros opens the door turning around he asks, "You coming Roxanne"? Roxanne, gives him the saddest look she could muster up, hoping he would stay and do something about those two under the tree, but he just said, "suit yourself", and with that Petros goes into the house leaving Roxanne alone to watch on her own the actions of her Adam and that female human! Laying down in the sun Roxanne let the sun's warmth over take her and she quickly falls asleep, there she is laying by her mom, safe and warm, then the next minute she was running down the dirt road and then BAM, Roxanne's eyes flew open confused, not seeing anything familiar around her, she frantically looks for that face that she knows so well, there he is sitting under that tree! Running to him, she didn't even notice Lydia or didn't care to, all she saw was her beloved Adam sitting there. When she finally noticed Lydia, it was too late, she was already airborne, leaping into what she thought was Adam's outstretched arms, but in reality were his arms around Lydia. As she crashed into her Roxanne let out a sort of whine/ growl at the same time and she landed perfectly in between Adam and Lydia, causing Adams arms to release Lydia and grab Roxanne! Unfortunately, Lydia didn't fare as well, with a startled cry; she landed on her backside, in the dirt on the other side of the bench! And Adam, well one minute he was looking into beautiful blue eyes, thinking that maybe he could actually share his heart with this lady and feeling very close and comfortable doing it, and the next he was looking into the very familiar and somewhat surprised eyes of his beloved Roxanne! Now it was Adam's turn to look surprised and confused! What is going on, he bellowed at Roxanne more harshly than he intended! You have behaved very badly Roxanne, "I'm very, disappointed in you"! Again Adam realized that he had said this with more harshness than he wanted, placing Roxanne on the ground, Adam turned to Lydia and offered his hand. I'm so sorry, Lydia, he said as he helped her up, "are you ok"? "Oh yes", she said, just a little embarrassed, that's all. Embarrassed, I'm the one that should be embarrassed, Adam said! I just don't know what has gotten into Roxanne, she is usually so friendly and loving. Actually, I'm very worried; she has been so strange since we have arrived here. First your mom and now you, Adam sat back down on the bench with this worried look on his face. Wait a minute, Lydia's eyes flew open wide, can I ask a personal question Adam? Adam just looked at her, "umm I guess so" he answered. Have you, um been friends with or had any female people around you, I mean since you've had Roxanne? Well, no, replied Adam, but what does that have to do with anything? Well, my dear Adam, Lydia said impatiently, as she took a deep breath, now all of this makes perfect sense! Adam just looked at her, now more confused than ever. Don't you see, Roxanne is jealous of any woman that gets close to you! She must feel threatened or that she will be replaced. No, Adam said, then he thought about it, do you really think that's the reason she's been acting so weird? With that comment they both bent down to look at Roxanne, who now was hiding under the bench afraid to come out, after Adam's scolding of her. Seeing both of them calling her and looking at her at the same time, made Roxanne feel more hurt and confused, so she moved farther under the bench. She was so confused by Adam's tone earlier, because he had never ever talked to her that way, angry like that, and it's all that female human's fault! She must be the kind that my momma used to warn me about, the bad ones! I want us to leave this place and never come back, so we never have to see that female again, Roxanne thought. Well, said Adam I guess she's not coming out, I'm afraid that I spoke to harshly to her. Lydia, may I sit here alone, with Roxanne for a while? Maybe she'll come out if I am here alone. Sure, said Lydia, I'll just go and help with dinner. You are staying for dinner right? She asked. Are you sure you still want me to? Adam said with a slight smile on his face. After all this, I wouldn't blame you if my bags were already sitting out on the porch! Now Adam, Lydia said laughing, don't even worry about it, you are welcome to stay as long as you like, and your bags are in the guest house, next to the shop. I'll show you when you're ready ok. And I am truly sorry about Simeon, I wish I could have met him. Thank you, Adam said he was like a father to me and I will forever miss him. With that Lydia kissed Adam on the cheek, turned and disappeared into the doorway of the kitchen, leaving Adam alone with Roxanne, who was still way under the bench, but very aware that they were alone now. Sitting on the bench, Adam sighed, well Roxanne he said, won't you come out now? Waiting, he hears or seen nothing. Finally he says, "all right, I'll just talk, and you listen". First of all, he started, I'm sorry that I yelled at you. I now understand why you have been acting so strange. Inching a little closer, Roxanne listens as Adam speaks. I need, no I want you to understand something, Roxanne there is nothing or no one that could ever take away what we have or my love for you, ok. It has been me and you from the beginning, and you have been my best friend that will never change. Looking down, Adam sees just a smidgen of a paw peeking out from under the bench, she's coming closer he thought, smiling. Then he whistles, come here girl, it's very hard talking to air, it's ok. Adam sees part of a black nose; he coaxes some more, then more nose, an eye and then the whole head. Finally, she emerges from under the bench, her small tail still and not wagging. Adam picks her up, and holds her close, no one will ever take that place in my heart that you fill, understand! Finally he gets a lick on the face and a tail wag. Ok he laughs; will you please try and give Lydia and her family a chance? They are very nice, and I sure like Lydia. Will you do this for me? Roxanne barks, well Adam laughs, I hope that means yes, because here she comes! So how is she? Lydia asks as she approaches the two. She's, fine, he replies, I think that we have come to an understanding, but more importantly, Lydia, how are you? I'm just fine, and dinner is almost ready, come on let me show you the guest house where you and Roxanne will be staying. As they made their way across the land over to the shop, Adam held on to her hand, and to their surprise, there were no protests from Roxanne. They stopped in front of a quaint little porch, in front of a quaint little door, and behind it, a very clean, modest guest house. Hope it is ok, Lydia says. Oh it's very nice, Adam replies. Over there is the work shop, where we make all the cloth, if you like I'll give you a tour of it after we eat. I would like it very much, Adam replied. Just as they were ready to step inside the house, Roxanne came running past them and flew into the room, jumping onto the bed, barking and wagging her little tail. Adam laughs, and turns to Lydia, I think this is her way of telling you she's sorry he says. Wonderful, Lydia says, do you mind if I have a moment alone with her? Not at all, Adam replied, now I'll just go and see if your mom needs any help with dinner! Turning to Roxanne Adam points a finger at her and says "now you be good girl ok! I'll be right behind you Lydia yells as she closes the door to the guest house. Alone with Roxanne, Lydia is not quite sure how to approach a jealous four legged female. So she decides to talk, like she would want to be talked to. Looking over at Roxanne, she sees her just sitting there looking at her also. Well Roxanne, she begins, we obviously have a slight problem between the two of us, that I think we can resolve. Do you agree? To Lydia's amazement, Roxanne barked and sat up, so she walked over to the bed sat down, and looking at Roxanne she begin to talk. I understand how protective you are of Adam and how much you love him. I would never try or want for that matter be responsible for hurting you or Adam or the bond that you two share. So please don't feel threatened by me. I have come to care for Adam deeply and I would love to get to know him better, but only if he feels the same and if I can win you over also. So, miss Roxanne, what do you say, do we have a deal? Will you give me a chance? Still looking at her at her as if she understood all that was said. Roxanne looked into Lydia's eyes as if she wanted to see her heart, and in her eyes she saw the same sincerity that she sees in Adam's eyes. So finally Roxanne felt at ease, she lifted up her paw and placed it into Lydia's hand, laughing Lydia shook her paw and Roxanne barked and licked her face. Ok, Lydia said come on now, we must get back to the house, it's been a long day and I'm very hungry, how about you? Again, Roxanne lets out a bark, and off they went towards the house and dinner and most important to Adam. " There you two are" Adam said sounding more relieved than he intended as Lydia walked into the kitchen with Roxanne right behind her. Everything ok? Adam asked Lydia softly. Better than ok Lydia replied. Good, Adam said I'm glad. Then they all sat down to a wonderful stew with Roxanne eating to her hearts content, under the table in between Adam and Lydia. So Adam, are you staying long? Petros asked a little too harshly. Father! Lydia started to protest, but before she could Rebecca spoke up, Adam is welcome here as long as he wishes, right Petros? Clearing his throat, Petros agrees,,,, of course, I was just curious that's all, looking down he mutters something no one could hear and resumes eating his stew. Now Adam, Rebecca continues, do you find the guest house comfortable? Oh yes, Adam replies, its wonderful thank-you, but I'll not stay here for free. Adam looks directly at Petros, sir do you have some work here that I may help with, to repay your kindness with? Until I can find what it is I am to do with the rest of my life that is he added. Looking up from his bowl, Petros replies," I am sure I can find something temporary around here for you to do. Good, it settled, now everyone eat said Rebecca, before your stew gets cold. After dinner was done and the kitchen was cleaned Lydia approached Adam, who was sitting outside with Roxanne. The sky was just starting to turn dark and the air was very cool. As she approaches, Adam stands, looking at here, he can't help but think as to how beautiful she is and he feels something in his heart, something that he has never felt before. Something strange and unfamiliar, but very good, and he could only think that he must be falling in love with this woman. Are you ready to take that tour of the shop now Adam, she says, interrupting his deep thoughts. I'm ready, Adam replies sounding more eager than he wanted, what about you Roxanne, Lydia asked as she looked down at her. Roxanne however was fast asleep, well I guess we will show her later, laughing they made their way towards the workshop, arm and arm. Lydia lit the lamp and they went inside the shop well, here it is, my father's cloth business, this is his heart and soul she said proudly. The room was quite large, with a section for washing wool, and spinning it and finally weaving it into cloth, all done by hand with great care. These over here are the weaver stands; the workers thread the string in and out and then push it down, pull this across and see, it causes a tight weave. They do this over and over, it's a fairly new way of doing things, but Father is very open to new and modern ideas. Adam whistled, I guess I never realized how much went into the making of clothes, it's amazing. Well, it's no armory, but it's ours, and were are proud of it. Over here, she grabs his hand and leads him to another room separate from the rest of the place and slightly smaller. Walking in you could smell the fragrance, strange smell, Adam said, sort of flowery and something else, but I can't place it. He looks at Lydia, but she just smiles, that my dear Adam, is my secret. In those tubs is my dye. I soak the cloth in three different kinds of dyes, to get that rich purple color that you were so impressed with. It's very costly, and time consuming, but in the end worth it. Yes I know that well, Adam said when I showed it to Simeon, his eyes lit up, he really liked it. I'm glad she said, as she turned to face him." I'm very happy that you came here Adam Lydia stared into his eyes. So am I, he replied, I really feel as if we have something special, and I would like to get to know you better, that is if you feel the same, Lydia. Adam stumbled over his words, but they felt right and he knew if he didn't say them now he might not ever say them. I feel the same way, Lydia answered, and I would be honored to get to know you better! For a moment, time stood still, and Adam would have been happy to just stay in that moment forever, but there was the matter of her father, who now was standing in the doorway, holding Roxanne, and clearing his throat, loudly! Lydia~! He bellowed, your mother is calling for you, and Roxanne was looking for you also sir! The moment had passed, and Lydia just smiled at Adam and said, "Ok papa", good night Adam, I'll see you in the morning. Good night Lydia, Adam replied, smiling himself, sleep well. With that, she turned and left Adam and her father alone, with Petros standing there, still holding Roxanne in his arms, glaring at Adam. Well, Petros sir, if you will be so kind as to hand me Roxanne, I will just excuse myself and head out to the guest house.

Petros gave no response, just stares, long, agonizing piercing stares! Now it was Adam's turn to clear his throat, and so he did, trying to think of the right words to say as he stood their face to face with the father of a woman he just may be in love with. And Roxanne, she gave no help at all, she also seemed to be staring at him, still and silent. So Adam began, Sir, I am not a youthful man, as you can see, and I am not a wealthy man either. The fact is I have never owned or lived in a house of my own, except for the brief time I lived with my friend Simeon. I don't have much money, Adam chuckles, well I really don't have any money to be truthful, but I am a hard worker, and I am an honest man. I have never been married and well, Lydia is my first female friend I have had, 'cept for Roxanne that is, and I feel such a strong connection with her, I'm so at ease with Lydia, it's like I have always known her and if you will give me chance, sir, I promise that no harm will come to her. If you allow me to, I will learn from you and her both all I can about the cloth making business, while Lydia and I get to know each other. But I will only stay with you and your wife's blessing, so tell me now, and Roxanne and I will leave right away if you so desire. Adam stopped talking, and took a long deep breath, and waited. Petros stood there, still glaring staring Adam directly in his eyes, and holding Roxanne, again that awkward silence filled the room. Do not look away Adam told himself, no matter how intimidating he gets! Finally Petros, looks away at Roxanne and begins to pet her, smiling ever so slightly he begins to speak. Well, he states, I did not have much when I met Rebecca either. Just my word, and a strong back, and as you well know Lydia is well, shall we say past the prime age of marriageability, and yes my Rebecca sure has taken a likening to you also, as for me well, I believe you when you speak of not hurting my daughter, and if you are what makes her happy, then I have taken a likening to you also! Adam straightened up a little, and his smile got a little wider, as Petros continued. I also really enjoy Roxanne's company, (Petros smile fades some) and I sure would miss her she left now, so sure I give you my blessing, for now! Just as they were getting ready to shake arm's on this new found if not shaky peace treaty between them Rebecca makes her way slowly to the door, Petros she orders, let this young man go to bed, it's getting very late. Adam, she turns to where she thinks she hears him breathing, can you find your way to the guest house alone? Yes, Adam replies, still smarting over Petros's comment that he would miss Roxanne more than him. Thank you both for all your kindness, and I will be here early to begin working sir. Petros just nods his head. Umm may I have my dog now! Adam says emphasizing the word" my" in the sentence. Petros, give the man his dog, so we can all get some rest! Rebecca chimed in, as she leans over feeling for Adam's face then she gave him a good night kiss on the cheek. Petros, hands over Roxanne, who whines a little enjoying all the petting she was getting, but settles quickly in her Adam's arms, board with all the drama that has been going on. See you early, was all Petros says to Adam before he and Rebecca turn, leaving Adam standing alone, well not totally alone, there in his arms, was his Roxanne, looking up with her loving eyes, as if to say, you don't have to prove anything to me, I love you just the way you are. Somehow just looking into that familiar furry face, he could sense those very thought coming from her, I know Roxanne, I love you too, he says in response, lets head to the guest house, it's been a long time since we've been able to sleep in a real bed eh! As he put Roxanne on the ground she readily agreed and ran ahead of him, almost before he could get her paws down on the ground! Running after her to catch up Adam did not notice Petros looking out of the corner of the kitchen window, with a very sad look on his face. Coming up behind him, Rebecca softly calls his name, causing him to get startled; he jumps slightly as snaps "Rebecca, you shouldn't sneak around like that"! "I almost turned around and gave you a punch, thinking you were an intruder"! "I shouldn't sneak", she sounded back, what are you doing peeking out the window anyway!. Sometimes it just amazed Petros at how perceptive Rebecca was even though she was blind. I may be blind, she continued as though she read his mind, but I know you all too well Petros Jonathan Thaddeus! You were spying, weren't you! I was not, Petros retorted, I was just looking to see if he had left and closed the shop door yet! Well, why wouldn't he you didn't exactly make him feel welcome in there, or all evening for that matter, she scolded. I only hope that he just went to the guest house and that he didn't leave all together. I think he is just what our daughter needs! Humph- we'll see Petros grumbles. Now Petros, you know Lydia is getting older and she hasn't many choices here, a traditional engagement and wedding have long since left her. I can tell in her voice how much she cares for him, and he for her. But he has nothing to offer her, Rebecca, Petros says with all the concern of a loving father. Petros, she touched her husband's face tenderly, he has his love, which is all you had when we met, remember? Yes, I remember, but we were much younger, and times were different then. Yes, she said, we were younger and not as wise as these two, Petros, all I ask is that you give him a fair chance, ok? Petros stayed quiet for a moment, ok I will, he said, kissing his wife's face, besides I've taken quite a liking to that cute little Roxanne! Now, he said can we please go to bed! It's late, and I need to be up early! Yes, Rebecca giggled tomorrow comes quickly, and holds a lot of promise for our daughter! Adam looks out the window of the guest house, then at Roxanne who made herself at home on the very large soft bed. Well, I guess we start over again eh girl? Roxanne gave a halfhearted bark and closed her eyes again, ok he laughs I'm tired too! As Adam laid there he thought of all that has happened these past few months, and how everything all lead him here, maybe, he whispered I finally can call this my home. Looking at the foot of the bed, seeing Roxanne, who now was looking at him with such love in her eyes, well what do you think, Roxanne, could you be happy if we stayed here awhile? Crawling up to his shoulder, Roxanne curls up under his arm and licks his face, laying her head on his chest, I'll take that as a yes, he says as he closes his eyes. Adam quickly falls asleep with a smile on his face dreaming of something wonderful. Roxanne just laid there for the longest time, just looking at her human friend, wondering if this is what her momma felt like when she had her family of humans, if so it feels wonderful! Seeing her Adam sleeping with such a peaceful look on his face caused Roxanne to be at peace also, I could be happy here, especially if Adam is, I might even come to love those female humans, which make him so happy! Yes, all is finally going our way; all is well, and with that in her mind Roxanne quickly fell into a deep peaceful sleep, dreaming of all the wonderful times still to come! Adam woke up early the next morning, and waited out front for Petros. He was eager to start the day and learn the business, so he could prove to Petros how hard a worker he is and prove that he is worthy of Lydia's love. Petros came outside, impressed that Adam was there waiting for him, but of course he did not show it, he just gave Adam a nod of his head and said follow me. And thus began Adam's and Roxanne's new life in a small town, in a small shop, with a new family! The next six months were full of happiness for both of them. Adam worked harder than he had ever worked in his whole life. After all he was working for something other than just wages or a roof over their head or food, he was working for love. Adam figured that the harder he worked the more Petros would respect and accept him into the family. Until Adam one day finally felt secure enough to ask Petros blessing for Lydia's hand in marriage! For a moment Petros just looked at Adam, again as if he were reading his very soul, then he spoke, " I know that my daughter is well, how should I say this, older than most, but she is my heart and my soul, and I have watched you closely these past few months". "I have watched you with my daughter and in your work, and I see the same devotion and honor in both places". Adam opened his mouth to speak but Petros rose his hand, "let me finish" he said. "As I said, I have seen the same love and dedication to both your work and my daughter, but when you are with Lydia I also see something different, such a look of peace enters your eyes when you look upon her, and I see such happiness in her eyes as she looks upon you"! And that Adam is something I haven't seen on her face or in her eyes in quite a long time, so I think my answer could only be yes, you have my full blessing"! Adam grabbed Petros's forearm and shook it vigorously, then grabbed him and gave him the biggest hug, thank-you Petros, I will live out my life making her happy! Petros pulled out of the bear hug and pointed a large chubby finger at Adam saying "you hurt her Adam, and I will never.... Adam interrupted him, you never have to worry about that Petros," only death will be strong enough to take me away from her" Adam vowed. Speaking of death, what about the other lady, Petros said, half smiling as he points to Roxanne sleeping under the tree where they had been standing and talking. Oh you know Roxanne, Adam says she's been very happy here and Lydia has been trying very hard to win her over, treats, walks, and such. I think as time progresses she will come around. I know she has become very close to you Petros. Yes, Petros says as he lets out a little snicker, never thought that I could grow so fond of a four legged creature the way I have your Roxanne! Well, Adam replies that seems to be the effect that Roxanne has on people. She wraps herself around your heart and stays there forever. So I'm counting that the same thing will happen with her and Lydia, it's just taking a little longer, but we are making progress, right? Just then, Roxanne woke up, sat up and looked first at Adam then at Petros, as if she heard and understood their whole conversation that just took place. They both looked at Roxanne, then at each other, then Petros laughed and said, "I will pray for you my son"! With that, he turned and left laughing even harder, "very funny" Adam yelled after him," I don't need prayers"! Then he looked down at Roxanne, looking so innocent, still looking up at Adam, he bent over and picked her up, petting her he hugged her and whispered, "I need a miracle"! The next day Adam got up earlier than usual, and took Roxanne out for a walk in the valley before the sun arose. He wanted sometime alone with just the two of them, and he wanted to gather his thoughts. After all his whole life was about to change, never again could he just pick up and leave, or sleep just anywhere. He will have a wife, responsibility, it was all a little scary to him, but he had never been more sure of anything, as he was of his love for Lydia, except of his love for Roxanne. So he felt he should spend some time alone with her, just them two, and maybe, try and see if he can communicate to her the changes that were about to come. As they watched the sun come up, sitting on the hill, Adam started to talk, like he always did to Roxanne, never quite knowing just how much she really understood, but talking about all that was on his mind anyway, if anything, it made him feel better, and she sure sat there and looked at him and listened like she would understand ever word he would say. Looking at her human that she loved so much, Roxanne could sense that he had a lot of emotion brewing in his heart, like he wanted to speak a lot of human words, but she didn't care, at that moment she was just happy to have him all to herself, without that female around, taking all the attention away from her. Now sitting here, on his lap, she remembered how long it had been since it was just them two. Still, it was not so bad here either, looking at Ada as he talks away and trying to sense what his words were, caused Roxanne to feel and see so many different emotions pass across his face, there was fear, uncertainty, love, and a lot of joy! Roxanne was glad to see that joy, it's been a long time since she had sensed such joy in him, and when Adam was happy, so was Roxanne. So for now she would just play, watch and get to know her new humans, making sure to especially keep an eye on that female one! As long as she sees that Lydia makes her Adam's eyes fill with joy, well that's good enough for her! For right now, at this moment I have him just to myself, so I am just happy to be here with my Adam, and soak up the warm morning sun, and listen....

# PART FOURTEEN; A HOME AT LAST

It had been four months since Adam had talked to Lydia's father and to Lydia herself, asking for her betrothal. He can still see the surprise in her eyes when she entered the workshop that night. He had lit up the whole shop with candles, and had set a beautiful table with all her favorite foods upon it, that he had spent all day in the kitchen preparing and the all-important glass of wine. The floor of the shop was littered with all kinds of wild flowers, which filled the whole room with a wonderful fragrance. As Lydia walked in the room and made her way down to the middle of the room, mouth open and eyes wide of course, there in the center of it all was Adam, in his best clothes, on his knees, and Roxanne sitting next to him dressed with Lydia's purple cloth around her neck, which is holding a single silver band! Adam smiled as he remembered the tears she shed as he spoke of all that was in his heart, and all the love he had for her, then he asked her to become his wife, so that the other half of his heart, which has been missing all his life could finally be whole. He had never felt such relief as he did when she smiled, took the glass of wine after he sipped it and said yes, and took a sip of it also, and just like that they were betrothed! And now here it is nearly a full year has passed since she utter yes to him and life was going very well. A wedding was being planned, Adam and Lydia were falling more and more in love, the business was progressing and busy. Adam and Petros seemed to be getting along very well, even Roxanne and the ladies seemed to be warming up to each other. There was much joy in the air, and Adam finally had a real home with a real family, which at times scared and overwhelmed him. Tonight was one of those times. It had an been especially busy day, as it always is when Passover time is nearing, all the hustle and bustle of people getting ready for it, brought the cloth business many orders and also they needed to produce extra regular and purple cloth to sell during Passover in the city. Usually Lydia made this trip alone to sell all the cloths leaving her family an making the trip to the city, but this time she will have Adam by her side, and that is what was making Adam so uneasy. Sitting around the table talking about the trip brought back many uninvited memories to Adam's mind that he thought he had dealt with, but obviously he hadn't because he could not escape them, no matter how many times he tried to push them away. So he excused himself, and went outside to get some fresh air, and to be alone. It wasn't long before Lydia got concerned and went outside, to check on Adam, with Roxanne close behind her of course. Adam, she said softly, as she saw him sitting under their tree, "are you ok"? Yes, he said, half smiling as he saw her approaching, I just needed some fresh air, and to think. Roxanne, sensing his distress jumps into his lap and sets her face in front of his, looking into his eyes with so much love for him, Adam could not help but smile. I'm ok Roxanne, don't look so worried. It's amazing how she knows when you are upset, Lydia said. I have never seen a human and an animal so in tune with each other as much as you and Roxanne are, she added. I only hope that with me added to the picture, Lydia continued, that it doesn't cause a wedge between you and her. Adam, is that why you're upset? The reason why you are out here, "thinking", are you having second thoughts? With that question, Lydia eyes filled with tears, even though she tried hard to steel herself for the answer. I mean she continued, with more fear in her voice than she intended, for she had come to love Adam so very much and the thought of losing him now was unbearable to her. The air was thick with silence, as neither one of them said a word, the she touched his arm and he looked into her concerned face, and loving tear filled eyes, and knew instantly what she was thinking. Oh no Lydia, he said I love you, he assured her with a hug and a kiss, please don't ever question that again he kisses her you are my soul and life, and don't ever forget that ok! Smiling, Lydia wraps her arms around his neck, ok she smiles, and as they hold each other closer, forgetting that Roxanne is also in his lap, until he hears a low growl from her, Both, Roxanne and Adam quickly let each other go and look down at a clearly annoyed Roxanne, causing them both to break out in a long loud laughter, at her expense of course! Well that just made matters worse, with what little dignity left Roxanne jumped out of Adam's lap and scampered back into the house, barley hearing Adam's yelling her name and their apologies in the distance! After they finally could bring themselves to stop laughing, at Roxanne's dilemma, Lydia asked him what was bothering him anyway. Oh, Lydia Adam said softly, just ghost's I guess. Ghosts? She asked. Well, it's just going back to the city, I haven't been back there since all that time with Simeon, and I thought I had dealt with it all, but now that were going back there, let's just say it will be a good time to finally deal with all those ghosts I have been hiding from, once and for all. Don't worry, Adam reassured her, everything is going to be fine, after all look at all the good that has happened. I have you, and I have you she answered him back smiling. Yes you do, Adam said, we have each other, a home a loving family and even Roxanne is happy here, look, Adam pointed into the house and there thru the window they could see Roxanne, sitting on Rebecca's lab by the fire, as she petted her and sang to her, looking very relaxed and happy! So much for her being mad at all women huh, Lydia said with a chuckle! Adam stood up, grabbing Lydia's hand, come on my love, let's go inside and join our family. Adam's smiled; I haven't had a family for a long time, sure feels good. Let's go inside, Lydia echoed as they both made their way back to the house. The road leading to the city was as busy as Adam remembered, when they were just outside of the city, again all the memories came flooding back, the cave, which thankfully they never came close to but they did stop by and pay their respects to Simeon's grave and still next to that was Roxanne's moms grave. Remarkably, Roxanne sniffing the small mound; remembers the scent of the flowers and trees growing wild around it. Bringing back memories of when she had smelled this scent before, pawing at the ground, she lies on top of it and waits looking at Lydia and Adam. As Lydia stands a little behind Adam, letting him have all the time he needs to deal with all his painful memories and "ghosts" as he puts it. Finally he stands, and turns around, are you ok, she asked; as she sees the pain in his eyes it hurt her heart more than she would have thought. I'm ok, Adam replied, I wish Simeon could have met you, he would have loved you. Well, from what you have told me about him, I believe that I would have loved him also,

Lydia replied, he must have been a very special man, to touch another's heart as deeply as he obviously has touched yours. He was, was all Adam replied, come on it's getting late let's get going, as they started to walk away Roxanne didn't move, she just stayed there, on top of her mother's grave. Turning around, Adam called her, she did not move. Why is she not coming? Lydia asked. Well, her mother is buried there, next to Simeon. Do you remember how I told you how her mom died and how I met Roxanne and why she has that lame leg and walk with a limp? Oh yes I do, poor baby Lydia said, may I go and get her? Sure, be careful I'm not so sure she wants to be bothered right now. Lydia walked over, Roxanne could see that female human coming over, if she tries to move me or picks me up I'll bite her! I don't want to leave my mommy, I remember these flowers, their wonderful smell, my mom, lying in the sun with her, I don't want to leave here again! Lydia did not try to pick up Roxanne or touch her she just sat down in the ground, next to the grave. Not saying anything; she began to pick flowers and placing then in a piece of purple cloth. Did you know Roxanne, she began that if you place many flowers in this cloth and leave them there for a while, and the oils from the flowers become part of the cloth, and make the cloth smell like the flowers? Pretending not to listen, but really watching and trying to understand everything she was saying and doing, Roxanne was not quite sure what her point was. So, continued Lydia if I do this with enough flowers from around here, we can take the smell that reminds you of your mom home with us, see! Holding the cloth open to Roxanne's nose to let her sniff it, not knowing how much if any of her words Roxanne would understand, Lydia was hoping that her nose would explain the rest. Sniffing the flowers, and watching this human putting them in a cloth, and picking up some familiar words, Roxanne finally understood what she was doing. Then something else came to Roxanne that this female human, was not trying to take her Adam away, she just wanted to be accepted and maybe she actually cared for me also! So Roxanne decided to accept her kind gesture, she crawled into Lydia's lap and licked her hand! Adam's mouth dropped open, and Lydia stood up with Roxanne in one arm and mess load of flowers wrapped in her cloth in the other! Are you ready to go into the city now Roxanne? Lydia asked.

Roxanne barked and licked her face! Ok then she said laughing, jump on the cart, and I'll wrap these flowers tightly, and place them in a press. Roxanne jumped into the cart, wagging her tail and barking happily. Adam scratching his head, asked Lydia, what in the world did you say to her to make her so happy, and what's going on with those flowers? Oh, Lydia smiled, we just had a girl to girl talk, I think Roxanne and I will be alright now. Well, Adam said still perplexed as he climbed into the cart, thank you, now let's get to the city and sell your cloth. You mean, our cloth don't you, Lydia replied. Yes, our cloth! Adam replied laughing. The great wall was as grand as Adam remembered, as was the city's gates, big impressive and seemingly unmoving. Are you ok? Lydia asked. Looking at her and seeing the love and concern in her eyes was all he needed, yes I'm great he answered, look, there is the heart of the city, let's start there and see what we can sell for a while at the market, then well get set up by the other cloth shop vendors ok. You're the boss! She replied. Roxanne barked, oh sorry Lydia corrected, after Roxanne of course! Laughing they quickly found a spot right in the middle of all the action, the day went very well, in fact sales went so well that they didn't have to stay the whole time that they thought they would need to, which suited Adam fine, all this noise and people made Adam very nervous and tired. As they were packing to leave, Lydia noticed how pale he looked and asked if he was ok. You look awfully pale, she told him, as she lovingly put a hand to his brow, maybe we should wait to travel and give you a night to rest, she stated worriedly. No! He stated, a bit more harshly than he intended, it's ok he added in a softer tone, really, Passover is finished, and I just need to get home, first time selling and all, just wore me out, that's all, I'm ok now, he hugged her, quit worrying really, let's just get packed up, I'm sure Roxanne is anxious to see your dad, they have gotten quite close you know, he said as he forced a smile. I've noticed that, Lydia said, does that bother you at all? She asked. Well, Adam said if I'm to be honest, I guess maybe a little, it's just that I never have had any competition, where Roxanne was concerned; it's always just been the two of us. Well, what about when you lived with Simeon? She asked. Was she not close to him? Yes, she was, but not the same way that she is with your dad. With Simeon, it was more a guardianship, especially after he

77

took ill, with Petros, it's more like they really enjoy each other's company, or something. Adam stopped loading the cart and looked at Lydia, sound's dumb huh? No, I understand, Lydia replies, by the way, you never did tell me exactly what Simeon illness was. Was it very painful? Adam's face turned paler than it already was, if that was possible. As he opened his mouth to speak, Lydia lifted her hand and put it over his lips to stop him, seeing the effect the question caused him. You know what, she said, never mind, I don't want to know, why bring up old hurts anyway. Come on let's get you home and this little one back to chasing the lambs! Adam smiled, and kissed her fingers, ok he said softly, grateful to not to have to answer her question. Come on Roxanne, he called lets go home! Looking up, Roxanne was rather upset at being disturbed from her adventure in the bushes behind the cart. She had never seen it before, it was long and thin, and it moved with such grace and precision along the ground. Just as she was about to sniff it, it would slither farther away, and make a strange noise that she hadn't heard before either. So of course being the curious sort and all that warranted her to investigate this strange object further, even if her Adam kept calling and calling her. Then Adam's calls became more demanding, so since she could no longer see that thing, she decided she better go back to the cart before he became too angry. As she was sauntering towards her Adam .Roxanne stopped cold, smelling a very faint, very familiar scent to her, she raised her nose to smell the air deeper, and the closer Adam got to her, the stronger that scent became, frightening her, as the scent gave her a feeling of a memory that was not good. There you are girl, he said as he bent to pick her up, she yelped and ran from him, into the cart and Lydia's arms! As she left Adam standing there, with open empty arms and a very astonished hurt look upon his face. What was that all about! Lydia asked as she struggled to keep Roxanne on her lap. I don't know, Adam replied, she was sniffing at the air and looked at me like she had never seen me before or something. Well, Lydia answered, maybe seeing you so pale frightened her. Adam just shook his head and shrugged his shoulders, maybe he replied, not sounding too convinced, and not wanting to think of it anymore, he put it in the back of his mind, he was just too tired to deal with anything right now. Let's go, he said, it's getting late. The ride home was a quiet one, each absorbed in their own thoughts, Lydia, busy with the sales figures, and of course wedding plans, and Adam, still wondering about Roxanne, why she acted so strange and wouldn't go to him. He admitted to himself at least, that it hurt him some to see Roxanne act that way towards him. But why, he wondered, she just kept sniffing and looking at him, what was that all about, what did she smell? I know I haven't had a good washing in a few days, but that has never bothered her before, and Lydia hasn't said anything, so what was it about his smell that frightened her so much he wondered. Denarii for your thoughts, Lydia said, breaking Adam's chain of thought, oh, he half smiled, just wondering how the sales went, he replied not convincing anyone that was what he truly was thinking of. I think we did quite well, he replied. Great! He said. Then silence. Lydia? He finally said. Yes? She answered. Do you, I mean, do I well, do I stink?! Lydia turned to look at Adam, blinked her eyes, and started laughing hysterically! No, she said in-between breaths, why do you ask? Well, it's just that when Roxanne wouldn't come to me, she just kept sniffing me a lot, like she could smell something, and that smell is what was scaring her away from me. Oh, Lydia tried to smother her laughs, as she said, Adam don't worry, she probably just smelled the city streets on you, and it might have brought back memories of when she got hit or something, you know how much she loves you Adam, you are her whole world! Maybe, Adam replied as he looked back at Roxanne, who was sleeping peacefully on a piece of cloth. He smiled, ok, maybe I'm worrying for nothing, and he smiled at Lydia, thanks for being my voice of reason. Anytime, she replied, I love you Adam. I love you too, Lydia. After they arrived home and unpacked, Adam bathed and Lydia washed all their clothes. Even Roxanne was back to her old self, not having any more episodes like the one in city. Time went quickly, and the wedding was fast approaching, only one month away. Lydia and Rebecca were very busy with all the final preparations. Petros and Adam tried to stay out of the way as best as they could, and Roxanne, well she just followed whoever would give her the most attention. Unless of course, when she felt the calling to chase the sheep around the land, to set the straight and let them know who's boss! Yes, it seemed like all was going very smooth, which made Adam very nervous. Never in his life had he been so happy, and had felt so much at home. One night as he lay in bed, he had turned in early, feeling more tired than usual, Adam thought about the happiness he and Roxanne had acquired living here, he remembered all the times that he had wished for a family and a home, and now that it is finally coming true for him! A smile came across his face, just think Roxanne, he said into the dark room as she lay there next to him. In less than a month, I will have a wife and you will have a.... what is that strange feeling on my leg? Adam's words were interrupted by a burning, itch one his leg, as he went to touch it the winced, as the area was extremely tender. Thinking that he may have gotten bit by some sort of insect Adam reached for the candle and moved his covers away to take a look at what was causing such a strange feeling on his leg. He touched his upper thigh again, ouch, what happened he said to himself, it's just so sore, and I don't see anything, he said confusingly, no redness or mark! Roxanne curiously came over and wanted to find out just what all the noise was about, seeing the distressed look on Adam's face, she sniffed the leg he was holding out, suddenly she again got that look of fear and recognition on her face, same as she did before, when they were selling the cloths, she whimpered a little and jumped off the bed and went and laid down in the corner of the house, looking very worried and scared. Roxanne, Adam said confused by her reaction, it's nothing, I just hurt my leg on something. Why are you acting this way? Adam go up from the bed and picked her up, holding her he whispered, "oh how I wish I could read your mind sometimes, I don't understand what you're afraid of, you have to know that I would never let anything hurt you, or anyone for that matter. So please trust me ok? Roxanne barked, Adam smiled, ok now let's get some sleep. The two of them laid back down with Roxanne quickly falling asleep, Adam however had a bit more trouble getting to sleep, heavy with many thoughts. In the morning Adam got up and went to the window to get a better look at his thigh in the light as it was still sore and feeling strange. In the light of day the area showed itself to be a rash, slightly red and patchy. Roxanne looked at him and him at her, "I know what you're thinking Roxanne and I am not going there!" Adam told her, with as much confidence as he could gather up. I'll just put some healing oil on it and it will get better, it's just a sore from a bite or something, just to be safe I will be careful not to be near anyone until it heals, to prove to you I was right! Everything will be fine, he said not sure if he believed his own words. Adam quickly went to the shop before anyone was awake and got some healing oils from the shelf and some covering for his leg, he knew that Lydia had kept it there for the workers in case of cuts and wounds. He covered his sore and dressed it with the covering, then he washed, got dressed, turning to Roxanne he says "now no one is to know Roxanne, this is our secret, no sniffing of my leg or acting weird around the family, ok! Roxanne barks and licks his face, as if to say, you're secret is safe with me! Putting on a happy face, Adam hoped that no one would see the fear and worry that he was trying to hide, in his eyes. Good morning Adam, Lydia greeted Adam as he entered the house. She opened her arms to kiss and hug him, turning his head, Adam moves Lydia away from himself, saying "feel like I am getting ill and I don't want to make you sick, sweetheart". Oh, Adam she says, "What can I do to help"? Can I get you something to eat? Lydia asked. No, he replies, I don't feel very hungry, I think I will just feed Roxanne, and then go for a small walk, ok? Sure, she said, trying not to sound hurt. Adam turned away as he called Roxanne to come, the he turned back to Lydia when he reached the door, looking deep into her eyes he said, "I love you, Lydia, I always will". I love you too, she replied. Adam? Yes, he said. Everything is going to be ok, isn't it she asked as she tried to search his face as she waited for an answer. Adam looking as confident as he possibly can for just as much his own sake as hers, he smiled, "of course it is. Now don't you have a wedding finish planning? Lydia smiled yes I have, but may I come by later and check on you. Sure he said softly as he closed the door behind him. Adam managed to avoid Lydia and elude all of them for the time that he needed, when she would come to check on him at the guest house he would pretend to be asleep, so she would just leave, not wanting to wake him. He felt terrible doing this to her, but he could not risk her life, till he was sure that they all were in no danger. This is it, he said to Roxanne as he removed the covering, this is the moment of truth! Barking, Roxanne jumped up and landed square on Adam's lap causing a deep pain to go thru his leg. He winced, causing her to lie down next to him, and whine. It's ok girl, it's not your fault, as Adam removed the rest of the covering, causing his worst fears to stare him in the face. That slightly red, nothing patch of skin, had grown into a very red angry open sore, with more skin sloughing off causing a smelly seeping wound! Panicking Adam looked at the rest of his leg, nothing there, he looked at his chest, nothing, turning he tried to see his side as he felt something, and there it was, another patch starting to form just like the first one! He could no longer deny the truth anymore, he had gotten what Simeon had and he too would suffer the same fate; pain and death! Falling to the floor, Adam cried out, "Why,why, was all he kept saying, finally raising himself up from the floor, Adam looks at Roxanne, who now was looking at him with eyes of concern and worry not sure what to do or how to help her friend. Adam knew that she would follow him to the ends of the earth if he would let her. Well, not this time he said to himself, he went outside and ground up a plant the grows wild, Adam knew his plants well and this one would put Roxanne into a very deep sleep, without any harm to her after she wakes up. After he ground up the plant he made a small treat for her with the leftover dinner that Lydia had brought him. He went over and sat beside Roxanne, "here girl, look what I made for you". Sniffing it Roxanne hesitated, not sure why the special treat was offered, but this is my Adam giving it to me, so she quickly at it all up. Now all Adam had to do was wait, holding her he talked to her letting her know how much he cared for her, finally her little body was very relaxed and limp. Adam knew that she had fallen into a very deep sleep, this was what he was waiting for, he needed to get as far away as he could, and he knew that she would follow him, so to make sure she couldn't he attached a tie around her waist and the other end to the post of the bed, the whole while speaking softly to her, "I love you Roxanne and I can't bear the thought of you seeing me go through the same thing Simeon did. You were so sad when he died, and I know how much you love me". But I love you more, more than the fear of being alone, besides, you have a home now with people who will take good care of you and who love you. Adam could no longer take it, the pain of losing everything was just too hard to bear, he placed a large bowl of water where she could get at it, covered her with his own shirt saying" so you know I'll always love you", then he placed a letter he wrote Lydia where she could see it. He knew she would be by to check on him, if he did not show up for breakfast in the morning. Grabbing the few things he was taking with him, Adam took one last look around. I almost had it all, didn't I girl, eyes filling up with tears he quietly turned and closed the door behind him, disappearing alone into the cold darkness of night.

# PART FIFTEEN; BETRAYAL

Why does my head feel so heavy? She wondered as she tried to clear the fog from her brain, and get all of her senses to working normally. Sniffing the air she tried to open her eyes, her lids feeling very heavy and her eyes very dry inside her lids. Roxanne tried to focus her eyes on something in the room; it was barley dawn so the room was still somewhat dark. She felt warm but she also felt something else, something she had never felt before, something around her neck, and it was very uncomfortable and itchy! Reaching her back paw up, she could tell this thing went all around her neck, confused, Roxanne looked around for her Adam, but could not see him in the darkened room, so she started to whine some, usually that would bring edam there quite fast. Waiting, but no Adam came to help her, so she tried to whine again, only this time a little louder,, then she waited again still no soft familiar voice of her friend. Felling now a little more awake, Roxanne jumped off the bed, and hurriedly headed towards the front door, only to get just half way and be cruelly and abruptly stopped by something that was attached to that thing around her waist, now she was really confused and she started to get very frightened. Where is my Adam, why did he leave me like this? Did he even know I am stuck like this, did he do this to me, is he ok? All these things started to take over Roxanne and overwhelm her and she began to remember her mother's words to her when she was very small "some humans seem kind, but in the end they mean you harm"! No not my Adam, Roxanne fought those feelings that he would actually do such a mean thing to her, she bolted for the door, causing the rope to yank her back violently, and landing her on her back on the floor, she let out a loud cry that even she didn't know she had in her, it was from deep inside, from down in her heart, then she just sat there, staring at the door, as if that act alone would open it. Time went on and nothing happened, the door did not open no matter how hard or how long she would stare at it. It was late afternoon now and Roxanne was, scared hungry and sad and very confused, then suddenly and without warning, she heard someone on the other side of the door. She sat up, tail wagging, it him I know it, I knew he wouldn't do this to me; I knew he would come a rescue me! Then a soft knock, a voice, Adam, it's me, are you awake? I let you sleep long enough sir, it's getting late are you feeling better, I was getting worried, Adam? Slowly the door opened, Roxanne barked excitedly, it him, he's home, then the door opens wider, suddenly her barking stopped. Roxanne couldn't understand what she saw, it wasn't her beloved Adam in the doorway ready to rescue her like he had so many times before, it was that female human, that Lydia! Crying loudly now, Roxanne just wanted to be free of her bindings so she could get away and look for herself for her Adam, so she started crying as loud as she possible could. Adam, Lydia said louder confused at why Roxanne was making such a racket, then she saw the rope and collar. Roxanne, what happened and why are you tied up? Quickly Lydia went to where Roxanne was, and started working on untying the rope all the time trying to keep the calm into her voice, talking to her and working to keep Roxanne from whining anymore, "it's all right girl" she said," Adam probably just wanted to be alone for a while, don't worry, he'll be back", she cooed, trying to convince herself as much as Roxanne. There, she said as she slipped the rope and collar off over Roxanne's head, does that feel better? Before she could finish the sentence Roxanne was gone out the door running down the road, quickly Lydia got up off the floor, running after her yelling her name but she was already gone, well she probably went to go find Adam, I'm sure they both will be back soon, she told herself, trying to dismiss that awful feeling she had in the pit of her stomach. Walking back to the guest house, Lydia went inside to take a look around before she closed the door; it was then that she noticed the rolled piece of papyrus on the table next to the bed bearing her family's mark on it. She did not want to notice it, to open it, but she knew she had to. Slowly she made her way over to the bed, it was as if someone else was walking over to that table, someone else was picking up that scrolled up note, that someone else slowly and carefully unrolled it, then recognizing the simple writing of

Adam, she started to read. Adam had told her that Simeon had taught him to read and write so that he could help with the smithy business, but it was very simple and limited, so she knew that he would write a letter that would be short and to the point. Slowly, as she wiped the tears from her face, she read the letter out loud. "Lydia, I will always love you, but I cannot marry you". "I now set you free of your commitment to me". Something happened, beyond both of our controls". Please be happy, I leave my only other love with you, Roxanne". Please love and care for her, I know that I have no right to ask this of you but she cannot come with me either. Thank you, for you gave me such love, and a home and happiness, that I have never known from another. I will never forget you, or your wonderful family. Adam". Sitting down, Lydia read the letter again, and yet again, trying to find some kind of clue as to what happened or where he went. Then when she could not deny the truth any longer, the tears began to flow, and flow, hearing a noise outside the front door she quickly ran to open it crying out Adam's name she flew the door open wide smiling, only to see and hear her father, saying, "no honey it's your father, your mother was getting worried so I came to check and see…. Petros then noticed the tears that were on his daughters face, what's the matter? He asked, fearing the answer as he noticed the empty room behind her. Lydia took a deep ragged breath, as she said the words out loud for the first time, handing her father the letter, "Adam's gone", there will be no wedding, the betrothal is over, the she just walked out into the fading afternoon, sad, confused and holding all the hurt and anger inside. Reading the letter, Petros ran after his daughter and into the house, screaming I knew he was no good, he told his wife as he stood and the base of the steps where Lydia was ! What is going on, Rebecca asked Lydia just turned and ran up the steps to her room. Petros, Rebecca said loudly, tell me now what has happened! Petros turned and faced his wife, "I'll tell you what's happened he said even louder than before, that man that you were so convinced was so good for our daughter,, just broke our daughter's heart! As calmly as he could Petros read the letter to his wife, when he finished, he just stood there crossed his arms, and waited for her reaction. There is a good reason as to why he did this, Rebecca calmly replied. "Yes! He's a coward! He ran away! Petros shouted. Keep your voice down, Rebecca scolded, Adam would not do this, unless there was no other way, he loved Lydia, I'm sure of it! Now I'm going up there to talk to our daughter, you try to calm down; she's going to need us, Petros, both of us! Lydia, Rebecca said softly, may I come in? He's gone mother, I chased him away! Oh Lydia, Rebecca maneuvered her way through the familiar room following her daughters voice, finding her by the window, she took her into her arms, sweetheart, she comforted her, you didn't chase Adam away, don't you realize how much he loves you? Lydia gave a sarcastic snicker and pulled away from her mother, sure he loves me, and love is why he snuck out in the middle of night, huh! Well, Rebecca replied, I'll admit it's rather strange, but think about it honey, why would he, just leave and not say good-by? Because he couldn't wait to get away from me Lydia retorted, through the tears that had started back up again. No! Rebecca stated firmly, trying to get Lydia to think beyond her broken heart and pain. Think, Lydia, he left Roxanne, would the Adam we came to know just leave her and do that without a good reason? Lydia, Rebecca said, I know in my heart, he will be back! For the first time since she read that letter, Lydia allowed herself some hope, do you really believe so mother? Yes, I do Rebecca said. Maybe all he needs is some time to himself, she added. Can you find it in your heart to wait awhile? Lydia looked at her mother, well, what choice do I have, I love him, there is nothing else I can do but wait and care for his dog..... It was then that Lydia's eye flew open wide oh no Roxanne! What! Rebecca exclaimed. What's the matter? Mother, it's Roxanne, it don't know where she is at! What do you mean? Rebecca stated with dread in her voice. Adam had tied her inside the guest house, I guess so she wouldn't follow him, but when I found her and I untied her, she took off! I tried to go after her but she was too fast, I really didn't think too much of it, then I found the letter, oh mother what if she ran away and we can't find her, or what if she is lost or hurt, we need to find her! Adam trusted me with her! Ok, calm down, Rebecca said, let's go get your father and we'll go and look for her. We'll find her don't worry, Rebecca consoled her daughter as they made their way down to the cloth shop and to Petros, who was working furiously, trying to forget all the anger he had inside for someone that he was beginning to think of as a son. She could not run any more, her lungs could not give her any more air, the road behind her, was just a blur, slowing down Roxanne sniffed the air, not smelling anything of her Adam, she just stopped right where she was, in the middle of the dirt road, sniffing deeper, frantically trying to smell something, anything that would lead her to Adam, not wanting to believe that he would just leave her all alone like that. Then suddenly she gets a faint sent of something, which triggers her memory, turning down the narrow side road the scent gets stronger, then its right in front of her! A squeal startled Roxanne, as she tried to stop, but she, but crashes right into a huge familiar pig and once again that familiar voice echoes in her brain. Don't hurt my sugar! Go away mean doggy! Oh no not a mean dog, Roxanne looks around. Go Away! The voice bellowed again as it got close to her. Holding a light close to her the voice yells "go awa… oh no, Roxanne is that you? Then the voice became a face and familiar smell that Roxanne knew and remembered, but it wasn't the smell or face that she wanted to see. What are you doing out here all alone? Still under Sugar's leg, Roxanne let out a whimper and tried to move the huge mass that was pinning her to the ground." Get up Sugar", Sephria said as she pushed on Sugar" and let up Roxanne"! A Squeal, protesting Sugar got slowly up and off Roxanne, as if to say "hey she ran into me"! Sephria picked up Roxanne, all the time talking to her, where is Adam sweetie, or Lydia? Why would they allow you out by yourself this late in the day when it is getting to be dark? You look so tired sweetie, come on, inside I'll feed you and you can sleep here tonight. Tomorrow I'll take you back to Adam in the morning. Too sad and tired to protest Roxanne just laid in her arms, not sure what the future held for her without her Adam in it. I can't find her anywhere, cried Lydia! She's not anywhere on this land! Just then Petros entered the home, looking very sad, Lydia and Rebecca looked and him,, he just shook his head, nothing, he said sadly. Well, Rebecca said softly, it's too dark and too late to look further for her tonight, we will start again in the morning. Lydia, sweetie try and get some sleep ok. Rebecca took her husband's arm, come dear let's go to bed. I'm going to the guest house, Lydia said in case she comes back there tonight. No one really slept well that night Petros and Rebecca were worried about their daughter, and Rebecca, tossing and wide awake, wondering and worried about Adam, where he was at, why he left, when or will he ever be back, and hoping that Roxanne wherever she is was ok. And then there was Roxanne, fed now and lying on the bed next to Sephria, so confused and hurt, not sure how to feel, abandoned, angry or just plain exhausted over it all, wanting so badly just to be next to her Adam and safe and warm by his side. With the rise of the sun, came a new day and a new hope. Petros and Lydia rose up early meeting Lydia in the kitchen still with a look of pain upon her face, just as they were getting ready to start their search for Roxanne again there was a knock at the door. Who that could be at this early hour, Lydia commented. Maybe it's Adam with Roxanne, cried Lydia as she ran to the door and flew it open only to see a familiar face, but not Adam's face. At first she just stood there holding the door open and staring, then she burst out into tears and ran past the kindly lady and out to the guest house, leaving everyone standing there looking at each other. I apologize for my daughter's in hospitability Rebecca quickly said to the woman standing at the door, "she is very upset". Yes I can see that, replied the lady. May I help you? Rebecca asked, slightly annoyed at this interruption into their plans. Yes, thank you, I am here to speak to Adam, is he available? Rebecca stayed quiet not quite sure what to say, Petros, however had to speak. Adam is not here, may I inquire as to who is asking for him and why? Oh yes, forgive me, my name is Sephria and I live down the way a bit and I found his dog Roxanne and….. Roxanne! You found Roxanne! Petros said loudly interrupting Sephria's explanation. Rebecca and Petros both invited the woman inside and started to question her, is she safe, where is she? Well, she's right outside the door, she was sitting at my feet. Petros ran to the door and looked out, no Roxanne, he looked towards Sephria. Oh my, she was just here, a minute ago! Roxie! Sephria begins to cackle where are you? Come here girl! Petros ran past the ladies and out the front door towards the cloth shop. Oh my, Shephria commented, he must really miss that dog, doesn't he? Yes, we all do, Rebecca said, would you mind if I take your arm and you lead me to where my husband is going, you see I am blind and I fear I will take too long to make it on my own. Oh my, my was all Shepria kept saying as she held out her arm for Rebecca to take, let's go sweetie and see just where that rascal Roxie went off to. As Petros turned the corner to the back of the house and headed towards the cloth shop, it was there that he spotted her, under the tree way under the bench, where she and Adam used to sit, looking like she lost her best friend was Roxanne! Bending down, feeling very much relief Petros softly called "Roxanne", "are you ok"? Roxanne didn't move or make any noise; she just laid there looking at him with those big brown eyes, full of hurt and sadness. Petros sighed, and sat on the bench saying, "I know you miss him girl, and I know you don't understand what's going on". I guess none of us do, but know this Roxanne; Petros sat back on the ground so he could see her eyes. Adam loves you, if he left you here; it was for a good reason. Roxanne, I love you too, Petros shook his big hairy head, I never thought that I would ever say that to a dog or could ever get so close to any animal this way, but there's something about you. It's like you give out so much love, he bent over to get as close as he could to her, will you trust me to love you back, to take care of you? That's only until Adam comes back ok? For a moment Roxanne could not move, she just laid there, feeling so scared and lost, then this familiar face in front of her, was talking in the same tone that her Adam would use. It felt good and right to her, so she came slowly out from under the bench, and crawled into Petros lap. Petros, picked her up and held her close to his heart, come on he said, let's go inside, and thank our neighbor for bringing you home safe.

# PART SIXTEEN; ON OUR OWN

She put the last of her things in her cart and took a deep breath before she had to go inside and say her last goodbyes. Hoping to gain some strength, she took another deep cleansing breath, because this was the hardest thing she will ever have to do, but she knew she could not stay here any longer, the memories to fresh and the hurt too deep; she just could not bear it any longer. Lydia stepped inside her home, standing there was her father, usually strong and gruff, his face now full of grief, his arms, holding tightly onto what has blossomed into the closest of companions, and best of friends, Roxanne. And next to him was her precious mom, Rebecca, holding onto Petros other arm, eyes though not able to see her daughter's face, are showing all her own pain and love for her daughter, with tears staining her cheeks. "Are you sure, Lydia that this is truly what you want to do"! Rebecca asks again, hoping to change her daughter's mind. "Yes, mother" replied Lydia I have to go, I can't bear to wait anymore. It's been too long. I know you still believe that he's coming back, Lydia softly said to her mother, but I cannot open that door at that guest house or sit on that porch staring out, only to see nothing but an empty room or a barren dry dirt road any longer. It's been over a year now, and it's killing me! I have to leave, to try and start something new, somewhere else new, to forget. The purple cloth business will help me make a new start, and you know that I won't be alone, some of the workers are going to come with me, Father saw to that! So don't worry, mother, I will be fine and in time, maybe I can even come home for good. Do you understand why I am leaving? Rebecca hugged her daughter, "I understand" she said and I love you, my daughter, Shalom. You will always have a home to come to. "I love you too mother" I promise that I will send word as to where I settle, and I will come back to visit you and father. Lydia turned to her father, taking Roxanne from his arms, she holds her tight, and whispers into her ear, "never give up on Adam, Roxanne, promise me that ok. Roxanne licks her face and give a low bark, Lydia continues, perhaps someday he will come for you, you truly were his best friend and I know he loved you more than his own life. Handing Roxanne back to her father, she give him a big hug, Lydia could not take any more of their looks of pain, so she hurriedly went outside, with her family close behind her. Climbing onto the cart, Lydia takes one last look at the entrance of the guest house, now door closed and locked up tight, then she looks at the barren dirt road behind her, and at her mother and father standing there crying, her father's arm around her mother's waist, the other one tightly holding Roxanne. Let's go she told the servant, the horses started to move and down the dirt road she went, trying but not able to even look back. The next few months were uneventful and quiet. Roxanne decided to stick close to Petros, so she followed him where ever he went, afraid to let him out of her sight, or he too might leave her like her Adam did. The Passover celebration was nearing, so Petros was very busy trying to get as much cloth .made to take into the city as he could. During the festival was the best time for them to sell, usually it was Lydia that would travel into the city and sell his and her cloth's but this year, it was up to Petros and his workers to accomplish this since Lydia has been long gone now for quite a while, and since he could not leave his wife alone, she too would accompany him into the city. Rebecca was excited about this trip; she had not left the house in quite a long while, and was so looking forward to getting away for a while. Of course where ever Petros went there also went Roxanne! The plan was to go about two weeks early and stay thru Passover, the city would be very busy so Petros had already secured a place to stay with some friends. It was the perfect place, really right in the heart of the city, perfect for cloth selling. As the time to leave drew nearer, Roxanne could sense that business as usual wasn't happening around her little world! I'm not too sure how Roxanne is going to deal with being in that city, Petros was saying to Rebecca one morning a few days before they were to leave. I worry about her running off, he continued, getting hurt; she's so used to the country now and her freedom. Well, Rebecca asked, should we leave her here? Petros shook his head; no I just don't have the heart to do that, not after what Adam has done already. You know, she still walks down to the end of the road every morning and stays there, while I tend to the animals. I didn't know that, replied Rebecca. Yes, it's so sad, she just sits and stares in the direction that, I guess she thinks that Adam left at, just looking, watching, sniffing, and waiting for any sign of him. It's really heartbreaking to watch, the after a while, she whimpers turns around and comes back home only to do it all over again the next day. So you see, I can't just leave her and drive away. No, I suppose that you can't replied Rebecca, then between the two of us we will just have to make sure she stays safe, ok! John reached out and held his wife, ok he said, it was then that he understood just how much he truly loved this women he was holding, and how special she was. The day had arrived, and the wagons were loaded, the sun was peeking over the hill, and the only thing left to do was to get themselves on the wagon and go. Petros got his wife settled and headed down, to get to the other side and get himself settled, well Roxanne was not about to be left behind, before Petros could even begin to sit down, she had jumped up into the wagon and had settled herself in-between Rebecca and Petros, barking and wagging her tail, and no one was going to tell her to leave or move or anything different! Well, Petros said with a laugh, I guess now we are ready! I guess so laughed Rebecca! So off they went down the dirt road, to the great city and hopefully a very prosperous Passover! He was holding her hand and walking in a field of wild flowers. It was so beautiful! She was so beautiful! Her hair dancing softly in the cool breeze, her eyes each having their own smile in them, how he loved her, he just wanted to stay in this field with her forever….CRACK his eyes flew open wide as the thunder rang across the sky. Realizing that he was only dreaming, Adam tried to adjust his eyes to the dim light in the cave, reality flooding his mind, along with the pain and stench of his present situation. Adam laid there on the cave ground on his homemade mat, just like the one he had made for Simeon all those years ago. As he laid there, thinking and trying to block out the fear he had of the future, as the leprosy had hit him cruelly and fast and the horrible loss of the past, he could not help but wonder what all of his family was doing right at this moment.

Did they forget about him by now? Did Lydia find another? Was Roxanne happy without him, content to love Petros instead? Thinking back, seeing Roxanne sleeping on the bed, how hurt and confused she must have been when she woke up the next day, leaving all that love behind, had been the hardest thing he had ever done, and the only place that he could think to go was back to the cave in the hills by the great city, the same cave that he and Roxanne lived and cared for Simeon in. It wasn't so bad at first, while he could still go out in the day light, at that time he did his best to prepare for later times. He hunted and stocked up as best as he could, and now that the disease has pretty much taken control, well he can still move, but with great pain and difficulty and not very fast either. CRACK ....the loud thunder continued as the rain came pouring down hard. Adam turned towards the fire, noticing that it was starting to die down; he took a deep breath, sat up slowly and with great effort and difficulty stood up. Making his way to the back of the cave he got some dry wood, his right leg dragging behind him, he guessed it was about late afternoon now, but didn't worry much about time anymore, because it was all the same to him now. All he was waiting for now and wanted now was for the peaceful release of death! Standing there at the mouth of the cave watching the pouring rain fall and the lighting flash across the dark clouded sky, brought him back to his family, it is getting close to Passover I think, so Lydia must be getting ready to go to the city to sell her and her father's cloth. Oh how I wish I could be there with them he said out loud, tears started to fill Adam's eyes as he thought of his love, Lydia and all that he lost. Just as he was deep in his own thoughts and pain, he heard a noise, carefully wiping away the tears, trying not to disturb any of the sores on his face, Adam listened straining through the wind and rain, it almost sounded like a dog barking.... He leaned closer to the outside of the cave, thinking he was imaging it he was just ready to give up when.....there it is again! It was not only a dog barking, but voices also! Grabbing his cape that he had received from a fellow leper, who left it to him after he had died, he wrapped himself completely up, for Adam had learned early on that his smell and look had not been welcome among the realm of "normal" people, now that only his eyes were showing as he slowly and not without some pain, made his way to where he thought he heart the barking and voices. Between the howling wind and pounding rain and the thunder claps, it was very slow going and hard to hear anything, but then he heard it again, yes it was a clear distinct barking of a dog and it sounded like it was just ahead! Trying to stay behind the safety of the trees and bushes Adam moved closer to the sound, finally getting close enough to see clearly, his eyes flew open wide at the scene ahead of him, he blinked, hardly believe what he was seeing before him, was this real or was he dreaming he thought! Pull the horses Levi! Petros bellowed to the man at the front of the wagon, who was one of the three workers that came along with Petros and Rebecca to help set up and sell their cloth. Levi pulled on the reins as the horses stated their complaints, and Petros and the other pushed at the back of the wagon trying to get the wagon out of the terrible puddle of mud which it was hopelessly stuck in, but to no avail, it just kept sinking in deeper. And Roxanne, well she was doing her best and loudest barking, trying to tell those horses to pull harder! That was the scene, which Adam stumbled upon and now was watching with disbelief. One minute he was feeling sorry for himself, and wondering about all of them and what they were doing, and the next minute here they are, right in front of him, so close to almost touch them! How he wanted to run to them, to whistle to Roxanne and hold her in his arms! To yell for Lydia, as he didn't see her or Rebecca he assumed that they were in the cart with the cover over it to stay dry from the rain, to explain to her why he left, to let her take him home and care for him, as he knows she would do without worry or question for her own safety. The rain had let up some, so Adam moved a little closer and settled himself behind a bush where he could stand and see and hear more clearly, it took all the will power he had not to walk out from that bush and reveal himself and end his horrible loneliness, but he knew he couldn't do that to them, no he loved them too much, so he just stood there from a safe distance, and watched and listened. Any luck? Asked Rebecca as she poked her head out of the covered cart. "No", Petros said as he huffed and coughed, standing upright for a minute he told Levi to stop and rest a moment while he looked for something to put under the wheel that would help give it some leverage. Petros, please let me get

95

out and help, Rebecca asked one more time, the rain has all but stopped and I can at least stretch my legs, I promise not to wander away, maybe I can even help push that cart a little, she said with a smile! Petros, chuckled and took in a deep breath,, "ok" he said, he never could say no to her when she looked so lovely or any other time for that matter! Petros held out his hand and helped his wife down out of the cart, he took her hand and put it on the rear of the cart, "hold on to the rope, I'm just going down the hill a little ways, to look for something the put under the wheel, ok". "Ok, Petros don't be such a worrier", Rebecca stated, "after all I do have Roxie here to protect me"! Hearing her name, Roxanne stopped her constant barking at the horsed long enough to run around to the back of the cart, where Petros and Rebecca were. Half way to there, she came to a sudden, dead stop, sniffing furiously at the air she turned toward the hills, looking and sniffing some more! Adam, noticing this bent down lower behind the bush and froze! It was as if Roxanne was looking right at him, and his heart started beating furiously! Sniffing again, Roxanne moved toward the hills and closer to Adam, and the scent that was so familiar yet not recognizable to her. She was sure she had smelled it before, but where, or who? And this place, she had been here also, if she could just cause her instincts to remember it, maybe if she found the source of that smell, she could remember what was so familiar about all of this. ROXANNE! Petros yelled out her name, come here girl! The voice of Petros, jolted Roxanne back to the present, she quickly turned around and jaunted back to her family, forgetting all about the strange, but familiar smell, worried about losing sight of Petros she ran faster back to him and into the cart that they had finally gotten free of the mud puddle. Finally, allowing himself to release his breath, Adam sat down on the ground behind the bush, watching his family slowly fade away down the muddy road as they resumed their journey towards the city. Sweet Roxanne, he thought, for a moment I thought that she saw me for sure, she was so close, I just wanted to hold her, tell her I was sorry for just leaving her alone, let her know why I did what I did. Adam wondered why Lydia never came out of the cart, or if she was even with them, maybe she decided to stay home this year. It probably was better that I not have seen her he thought,

I could barely stand to see Roxanne, Petros and Rebecca. I don't think I could bear seeing Lydia, why Lord, why did this happen, Adam cried out loud, "was I such a bad person, that I deserved all this pain"? After he sat there awhile, he gathered all the strength that he had left, and pulled himself out of the mud, slowly he went back to his cave, sadder and even more defeated than when he left earlier, wanting death to come now even more than he did before. In the cave, laying down now by the fire, Adam again thought about all he had seen today, and he wept bitterly for all he had lost, until there was nothing left in him to cry out, then he finally fell into a restless sleep, thankful for at least being able to see his family one more time, even though he wasn't able to see Lydia, knowing that they were all ok, he finally was at peace with his own destiny with death. By the time they reached the great city gates they were all very tired, wet and cold, so Petros found their friends house first without searching for a place to set up their items of cloth, which normally they would do first, so they could secure the best possible place for selling. Petros could see the weariness on Rebecca's face so he opted to get her inside somewhere warm and dry first. Finding the house was very easy, and his friend was expecting him, welcoming all of them with open arms and warms smiles. "Shalom my brother it is so good to see you my friend" Josiah said as he gave Petros a great big hug. "Shalom", Petros replied back, "I am very happy to see my old friend also". Petros and Josiah had been friends since childhood, both had studied together in the temple schools, and had planned to open the cloth business together, but Josiah had a different calling and wanted to stay in the city. He thought, he would be a great Pharisee but ended up being a servant to them instead, which to Josiah was just fine, he was a humble and honorable man, happy just to be part of the great temple. After patiently waiting quite a while, Rebecca finally cleared her throat, bringing Petros back to the present! Oh forgive me, he went over and took her are, Josiah, he said with pride, may I present my wife Rebecca! Josiah took Rebecca's small hand into his very large one, ahh yes he said "I remember you lovely face"! "You are as beautiful now as you were on your wedding day", he added! Blushing Rebecca smiled, "you are too kind" she said shyly. Suddenly a young lady comes running out of the door just as Josiah was showing his guests into his home, almost causing Rebecca to lose her balance and fall! Child, Josiah sternly corrects, "Our guests have arrived"! Stopping cold in her tracks, the young lady walks slower to her Josiah's side. She appeared to be in her late teens, early twenties, thought Petros, but he didn't think that Josiah had any children or ever gotten married. Then Josiah spoke, Petros, Rebecca, may I introduce to you my niece, Veronica! She and her aunt live just outside the city, and they come here often, to help me with the household chores and such, I don't know what I would do without this little one's help! "Oh uncle" Veronica smiles, and then turns her attention to Petros and Rebecca "it's very nice to meet you both" she said politely. Shalom they both replied, smiling and hugging the girl. "Come", Veronica said, you must be exhausted, let me show you to your room. Yes, exclaimed Josiah, you two get settled, and I will get your workers and horses settled in the stables. Just as they were headed to the upper area of the house and to their room, Roxanne came barreling thru the front door and flew into Petros arms, determined not to be left behind! And who is this, exclaimed Josiah, laughing. This said Petros, as he adjusted her in his arms, is Roxanne, we sort of inherited her from a friend of our daughters. Well, she sure seems attached to you, Veronica said. Yes, Petros said, she rarely leaves my side, I suppose she is still missing her original master, so when he left she became afraid that I would leave also. Then I guess we need to set up a little place for her in your room don't we, Veronica answered. Well, Petros, Josiah chuckled, you old softie, I have never known you to be such an animal lover! Well, Petros said blushing slightly, Roxanne here is very special, and she's practically human, aren't you girl! Looking at Petros, Roxanne gave him the best most soulful, understanding look and then proceeded to place a very wet, very long lick from his chin to his forehead causing everyone to breakout laughing, everyone that is except for Rebecca, who felt left out of the whole experience because of her blindness. See what I mean, Petros said in-between his chuckles, I do said Josiah, come let's get you all settled in. The morning comes quickly in the city. Once in their room, Rebecca remained unusually quiet, when Petros would ask her what the matter was, she would just say that she was tired, but he knew something more was wrong. For the first time Rebecca was feeling isolated, and sorry for herself because of her blindness. As they were laying there that evening, waiting for the new day, Petros anxious for a good sale result, Rebecca having second thoughts about coming, and Roxanne just happy to be by Petros side, no one really prepared for what was actually was going to be an experience they will never forget!

# PART SEVENTEEN; THE GIFT

The morning did come quickly and full of sunshine. Petros was the first to wake and get downstairs, he was eager to find a location to set up his shop so he went walking around the city looking, before anyone else had claimed any more spots, with Roxanne by his side of course. The City was just beginning to come alive, with a few people and as they made their way down the dirt road, Roxanne being around all the smells of this city and seeing all these houses and shops, started to get strange sensations, then as they passed this old broken down burned out building, her memories came alive, and she remember this city, suddenly running ahead of Petros, she ran into the old building, barley hearing the cries of Petros for her to stop. Running thru to the other side Roxanne stopped at the place where her and Simeon and Adam would sit for hours and laugh and talk, it was what used to be the front porch, but for Roxanne it was all the memory she needed to bring all her past back alive, her mom, and her living just beyond those walls, in the hills, how she first came to meet her Adam. Roxanne walked out to the middle of the road, sniffing she also remembered how she hurt her leg that day and why she now has always walked strangely ever since. Sniffing and pawing at the dirt road, she gave a whimper and looked up to see a figure running from the back to the front of the ruined shop calling her name. It's him! It's him! He's come back for me! Running as fast as her limp would allow her she headed full speed towards the man headed in her direction, barking furiously all the time, as she got closer she came to a sudden stop a few feet before Petros could catch up to her, and just sat down, knowing now that it was Petros and not her beloved Adam that was calling her. Roxanne! Petros cried as he got closer to her, "what got into you"? "Why did you run to this old place"? It's ready to fall down and you could have gotten hurt! Before Petros could gather up Roxanne and leave the ruins a voice yelled at him from the street, "Hey, you what are you doing there, you should not be on this land!" Petros looked up after he picked Roxanne up, much to her protests, and quickly approaching him was an old solder, he stood right in front of Petros, fists clenched and was quite angry looking. Quickly, Petros explained that his dog had ran into here and he was just trying to catch her and now that he had, he was leaving, he said that he was sorry if he caused any harm and he won't be coming on this area again. All the while trying to say this above the low menacing growls coming out of Roxanne! Well, the solder said a little softer, no harm done, and this place is going to be torn down soon anyway, it's been marked for destruction for years. The owner only has a few days left to claim it, before it belongs to the city probably to be demolished and sell the land for back taxes if figure. May I ask what this place used to be, Petros asked the stranger. Oh, it used to be a blacksmiths shop, quite a busy one as I recall, till the owner came down with the unclean sickness like those lepers outside the city, the whole city along with a few roman soldiers drove him away, along with everyone else that was living with him. Then they tried to burn the place down, it's been this way ever since. That is a sad story, Petros thought, I wonder why Roxanne insisted on coming thru this old place, it's like it was familiar to her or something. Anyway, the old solder grumbled, interrupting Petros's train of thought, you need to move on! Yes, Petros said, were leaving right now, let's go Roxanne, this is no place for you, Roxanne let out a small whimper, as Petros turned to leave, carrying her away from the first place that had opened a floodgate of memories about this city and its surroundings, bringing the pain of Adam to her heart, causing her to once again wonder where he was and why he left her the way he did. All she could do is watch as the ruins of her former home got smaller and smaller, but the other places in the city, well they started to grow in her memory, the streets, the smells, especially the smells, she could smell the scent of horses, which reminded her of the pain of when she was got hit in the road, just over there, she can smell and see the market place now with all the wonderful foods and items, and it reminded her of Adam and Simeon and all the times they would walk thru the market place, and she would do tricks for them and they would laugh and sometimes give her special treats! Roxanne let out a loud whine, startling Petros. Roxanne, Petros stopped walking so fast and adjusted her in his arms, are you ok? He asked. Did I hurt you? She just looked at him, with such sadness in her eyes, all he could say was you look as tired as I feel, because he could not even begin to understand the sadness that those eyes were trying to communicate to him, come on he told her lets go back to Josiah home, tomorrow is going to be a very busy day and I'm sure that Rebecca is probably getting worried by now anyway. That night Roxanne sleep was very restless the memories just kept coming, that night more than any other for Roxanne, and she missed Adam something fierce, she felt him near when she was here, and was more determined than ever to find him, somehow she just knew that he needed her badly, why or where she knew not, but find him she would! Finally falling asleep, determined that her Adam soon would be home, because she would bring him home. Everyone was so busy the next morning trying to set up for the cloth sales, that no one noticed when Roxanne slipped away as they were setting up their carts and cloths at the sight that Petros picked out earlier. She ran down the road towards the place where she, Adam and Simeon lived, the place where a lot of her memories were at. Walking thru the old partially burned out old house, she started to smell familiar scents, faint though they were, they still were present and caused her mind to trigger memories, here in what was the kitchen, them laughing at her as she would eat her meal with her face full of stew gravy, and there in that old dirty chair is where Adam would hold her for hours and the two of them would just bond, he would tell her all his troubles while he brushed or petted her. Roxanne carefully climbed into the old chair and just lay there awhile, desperately trying to see if just a small scent of her Adam remained in the chair. But all she could smell is dust and old mustiness. Jumping down sadly she went into the last room, Simeon's room, and the Stench of sickness and death was still present here in this room, Roxanne remembered just how long that scent of death she had smelled for and how it had gotten stronger as Simeon had gotten worse, this scent was and will always be strong in her mind, it brought forth a memory that was more recent also, one that did not take place here, Roxanne went farther into the dark room, still there in the far corner covered with dirt and debris was the small bed that Simeon had slept on, as she took a very long very detailed smell of the bed which still had much of the same stench of the sickness on it, causing her to realize just where else she had smelled that same thing, out on that road, when we were stuck in the mud, just a few days ago! Sniffing again Roxanne realized that the scents were the same and maybe just maybe it would lead her to Adam! Turning and running as fast as she could Roxanne left the house and ran towards the Great entrance gates of the city being careful not to get in the way of the people or the horses as she left the city and started going up the dirt road a lot was starting to look very familiar to her, remembering her life in the cave and the reason why they left the cave, and then she saw the mound remembering her mother grave and Simeon's also, not stopping to sniff or rest beside them Roxanne ran past the graves and past the olive trees up the hill in hopeful anticipation of finally finding her Adam there. Hardly being able to catch her breath Roxanne turn's the last curve, that same familiar scent growing stronger with each stride closer that she gets towards the cave that she and Adam and Simeon spent their last times together at. Seeing the cave's entrance, Roxanne runs inside barking furiously and wildly then she stops and listens, the darkness yields no noise back, just the whistling of air thru the endless blackness. Walking further, Roxanne sees something against the cave wall, walking over to investigate the shadow finding a blanket and a few pieces of stale old bread. Walking farther into the darkness, more cautiously now, Roxanne lets out a low quiet bark, letting anyone or anything inside the blackness know that she was here and meant no harm. Suddenly she hears a low menacing growl that makes her hair on her back stand up! As she takes another step forward the growl gets louder, and that scent so much stronger now, one more carful step closer, when out of the darkness, comes something that hits her right on her left shoulder startling her so much that she lets out a loud yelp that echo's down to the bowels of the cave! A loud more menacing growl answers her. More afraid beyond what she can take Roxanne turns to leave just as something else pokes her behind! Well, that was all she needed, yelping even louder with every step she took, Roxanne ran toward the mouth of that cave, never looking back and never stopping until she was back safe inside the city gates!

Adam watched as she ran down the hill, out of sight with tears streaming down his face and filling the putrid, rotting holes on what was left of his cheeks. Convinced he did the right thing, he looked around the cave making sure that he had gotten up all the things that possibly would have triggered something in Roxanne's mind that would give her the idea that he was there in that cave. He could hardly believe his eyes earlier when he was sitting on a rock, trying to feel the sun on his face so possibly some of the awful sores would dry up, in hopes that it would lessen some of the pain, when he saw far off a small creature running in his direction. At first he thought it was a wild boar or some such animal, so he just sat there watching it. Then as it came into clear focus, well Adam blinked and blinked again, then he leaned some to get a closer look, why it looks like…. No it can't be he muttered. Closer and closer the figure came, yes he said with excitement, it is! It's Roxanne! Adam got slowly to his feet, feeling every movement. I can't let her see me, I just can't! He said sadly out loud. As quickly as he could he went inside the cave and gathered all he could and placed it all upon the small mat that he had made for him to sleep on and moved far back into the black darkness of the cave's interior, pulling along his small mat. He barely made his way back there when she entered the mouth of the cave barking like a crazy dog! From where he was he could clearly see the cave's entrance and a few feet inside. I must scare her away from here so she will never want to come back, he thought to himself. I cannot put her through another death like Simeon's, I love her too much, I love all of them too much, so Adam started to growl low at first then louder. He tried to make it sound as frightening as he could, when he saw that she was still determined to walk forward some more he got a small stone and tossed it lightly hitting her shoulder, that seemed to do the trick, but Adam wanted to make sure she would never come back so he poked her softly on the behind, with a long stick that he used as a walking stick, and knowing his Roxanne well that was all that she would need to get her to go and go fast. Finally safe inside the city's gates Roxanne tried to catch her breath, when she heard someone call her name, turning around she gazed upon a man who had the kindest eyes that she had ever seen, kinder than even her Adam's! "Roxanne" He said softly," what are you doing way out here, shivering by the gates"? Gently the man picked her up and held her close, immediately Roxanne's shivering stopped peaceful now she laid her head in his arms totally relaxed. "You know this dog's name, Teacher"? The man next to him asked. Yes, he answered, Roxanne and I have met before haven't we girl! Come, he said let us take this little one back to her care givers, she still has some unfinished tasks to complete. But, teacher, the man answered as he pointed to a large gathering of people that was beside them, "there is a large crowd following us, dare we leave them for just one of these small creatures"? The man holding Roxanne smiled and put his hand on the shoulder of the his friend, "my Father loves all his creations, the people will understand and follow and see proof of my Father's love"! So Roxanne, who was extremely content in this man's arms, and all who followed him headed towards the little wagons, in the heart of the city, where Petros, Rebecca and Josiah were preoccupied and busy with the selling and trading of their cloths. Hearing a commotion and seeing such a crowd of people coming down the dirt road, Petros moved out from behind his cart and looked down the road to see if he could tell what was going on. He could hardly believe what his own eyes were seeing. A man he had never seen before was holding Roxanne of all things, and they were being followed by a large crowd of people, just laughing and dancing. "I don't believe it"! Petros exclaimed as he rubbed his beard and shook his head. "What is it Petros?" Rebecca asked. For she too could now hear the laughter of people and knew that there must be a large group approaching. Taking her husband's arm, feeling slightly afraid Rebecca asks again, "what is all that noise and chatter, are there solders coming"? She asked fearfully. Don't be frightened, he said squeezing her hand, it's just Roxanne and some new friends she must have just made. Just as he was getting ready to describe to Rebecca the scene before him, Veronica came running up the road and past the wagons, past Rebecca and Petros, yelling "it's him, it's him"!" He's finally come back, how wonderful"! As veronica and others ran up to this man and fell to their knees, Petros turned to Josiah and asked. "Who is this man"? I don't know, Josiah answered, but seeing the reaction of Veronica and those others he must be someone very important. The closer the man got to them the faster Petros heart would beat, causing his legs to weaken, holding her husband's arm tighter, Rebecca could sense that this person coming towards them was no ordinary man. "Peace be to you", he said as he stopped right in front of them, immediately Petros felt a calming and ease in his heart and body. "Shalom" Petros answered. "I believe this lost dog is entrusted to your care"? The man said smiling as he held out Roxanne. Petros tore his gaze away from the man's piercing eyes to look down at the totally relaxed Roxanne, sleeping peacefully in his arms. Ummm why yes sir, she is he stammered. May I ask, where you found her? "She was out there, just inside the city gates". He replied as he pointed down the road. Oh my, Rebecca cried, Roxanne what in the world caused you to wander so far away from us?" I believe this little girl was out on a quest", the man answered, matter a factly as if dogs everywhere go out on quests all the time! Well, Petros said as he took the rather reluctant Roxanne from the man's arms, thank you for bringing her home. Then Veronica asked him if he would please stay with them awhile, and teach them. He replied that he was going to be staying at the home of a tax collector, which caused all four of them to give each other a curious look, not understanding why anyone would want to do that! Then he patted Roxanne's head and told her not to give up on her quest, to follow her heart, listen to her instincts and they will lead her down the right path. Roxanne barked as if she understood his every word. As he started to walk away, the large crowd of people following, he heard a small voice call out. Teacher, Master? The man turns and sees Rebecca, standing in the middle of the dirt road, still holding onto her husband's arm, who also still has hold of Roxanne in his arms. On the other side supporting Rebecca was Veronica and Josiah. Teacher, Rebecca called out again. Yes, daughter, what is it that you want, the man asks softly as he turns to face her. "Veronica tells me that you are a prophet, the holy one". She says very, very softly, with her eyes facing the ground. "And what does your heart tell you". He asks as he lifts her face upward. "I see in my heart that you are who you say you are, and I do believe"! She says this time much louder and with great confidence! He smiled and said "then not only shall you see with only your heart, but also with your eyes, because you believe"! He touched Rebecca's eyes, and she gasped loudly as immediately a bright light flooded her eyes, then it became different colors of blue and reds and yellows, then blurry forms started to come to focus, then she saw them, the most beautiful incredible pair of eyes, so kind looking back at her! She fell to her knees, taking in all of the beauty of the earth, the dirt, the rocks the sky, the whole world that had been denied her for so long, crying all she could say was a humble, "thank-you". The teacher bent down to the student and lifted her back upon her feet, he smiled and kissed her cheek and said "your Father in heaven loves you, which is why I came, to show you all just how much He loves you"! Then turning he disappeared into the crowd and he and they walked farther down the road towards the temple. Now, standing there alone still holding on to Roxanne, mouth wide open and not quite sure just what took place, was Petros. Turning, he looked at his wife, still standing in the middle of the street, she turned and looked at him, really for the first time looked at her husband, her face was radiant, and more importantly her eyes were focused on his! For a moment Petros stood there, letting it all sink in, finally it all connected and a smile as wide as his ears caused Rebecca to start laughing, and Roxanne to start barking and howling. He grabbed his wife in one arm and spun them all around laughing and crying and singing all at the same time! That night they had a huge celebration, with Roxanne on Rebecca's lap as the guest of honor! As they figure, if she would not have gotten lost, then the Rabbi would not have come to them, and Rebecca would not have gotten her sight back. As they celebrated, Rebecca's thoughts turned to their daughter, as she wished that she was here with them to celebrate. That night after everyone had left, Petros, Josiah Veronica and Rebecca were sitting on the roof, along with Roxanne of course who was sound asleep, exhausted after all the day's events. I wish Lydia were here, Rebecca said sadly, breaking the silence of everyone's deep thoughts. I do too, replied Petros, still trying to get used to the idea that Rebecca can see now. Petros, Rebecca suddenly sat up her face lit up, if she can't be here, why don't we go to her? "What are you saying"? He asked afraid of the answer. You mean leave here, now so close to Passover, and miss all the potential cloths sales? Rebecca looked disappointed, "no I suppose that would not be wise". She concluded. You don't have to miss anything! Josiah chimed in, "you can leave everything here and I and your workers will see to the sale of your cloth"! You would do that for us? Petros asked. Of course, your family! Josiah answered smiling. And besides, your wife is a walking miracle now, who am I to stop her from spreading her good news! Josiah chuckled. Just then Roxanne woke up and jumped into Petros lap. And what of her? Do we drag her all around with us? Petros asked. Lydia closed her bright beautiful eyes, she could think better in the darkness, she knew that Roxanne would travel fine, but she wasn't sure if Lydia would be fine seeing Roxanne. Would this cause fresh wounds to re-open? She just didn't know, she hadn't heard from her in a while, only that she was fine and were she was living and that she had started up a new cloth business. She said nothing about how she was doing in her heart, or how she was feeling about the whole Adam thing. So she explained her fears to the rest of them. Well, veronica said I really love Roxanne, and I don't think Josiah would mind keeping her in his home, would you. Josiah readily agreed, "not at all "he said, "She is very well behaved, most of the time". "I don't know, Petros said rubbing his beard again, what if she runs off again, I would never forgive myself if she got hurt, or worse. Petros, Josiah went over and took Roxanne from his lap, I give you my promise, I and my family will take very good care of her, ok! Petros looked over at his wife, her eyes now full of life and expression pleading to him, without her even having to saying anything. Well, he finally said, looking straight at his beautiful wife, a twinkle of his own in his eyes, I guess we are off again to visit our daughter! Running over to him, Rebecca gave her husband a huge hug, thank-you she said. For you my love, anything, now let's get back to the house, we must get some sleep if we are to pack and leave at a decent hour tomorrow, Petros commanded smiling! The next morning they were all up early, with Rebecca leading the way, with the packing, used to doing it his way Petros was going to have to get used to a lot of changes, now that his wife's sight was back, but he was happy about each and every one of those changes, except one, and that was his looks. Now that she can see him, he wondered, was she disappointed in the way he looked? She is so beautiful and he, well, he was just Petros, as he sat there in the room, lost in his own thoughts, Rebecca entered the room and saw the look upon his face. Petros, she said, are you alright? Come, he said holding out his hand, sit with me a moment. Rebecca sat looking at this man that she loved so much but haven't seen what is it? She asked worriedly. "Are you, he began stumbling over his words, "I mean now that you can see me, are you well, are you disappointed?" Petros looked down, almost afraid of what answer she might give. Petros, Rebecca said softly, he looked up at her face, "you are and always will be my husband, my best friend, I love you, and she continued, I especially love that handsome face of yours!" Seeing your face was the most precious sight I ever will see, ok! OK, he repeated his cheeks slightly blushing, now then, he said let's go and tell our daughter our wonderful news! After you explain it to the other lady in your life, Rebecca said as she pointed to Roxanne who was sitting in the doorway watching the two of them. Oh yes, Petros took a big deep breath, I'll meet you outside, give me some time alone with her ok. As Rebecca left she picked up Roxanne and gave her a big hug, I will miss you, please stay safe till we get back. Roxanne, just licked her face and Rebecca gave her over to Petros. Well Roxanne, Petros began, we need to talk, and I need you to listen very carefully, try and understand how important this is to Rebecca ok. Roxanne barked and wagged her tail, then Petros proceeded to try and explain to her what was about to take place and why they were leaving and not taking her along. Roxanne watched as another person left her. Veronica held her in her arms, trying to console her and letting her know that they would be back very soon to get her. But somehow Roxanne knew this not to be true, as she watched Petros get smaller and farther down the dirt road, but this time it was different, there was a joy and peace in all their lives since the teacher had visited and healed Rebecca of her blindness. So Roxanne was ok being left behind, she was at peace, she sensed that she should once again wait for her beloved Adam to return for her or for her to find him, she felt him near and somehow knew that he needed her desperately. Come on Roxanne, Let's go inside and get you something to eat, Veronica said after the cart was far out of sight. But food was the farthest thing from her mind right now, all she wanted to do was sit and wait that's all.

# PART EIGHTEEN: ANTICIPATION

Time passed by quickly for Josiah and his family, Passover was approaching fast and the city was getting very busy and crowded. They all were working very hard to keep Petros's business going strong and to try and keep a close eye on Roxanne at the same time making her feel loved and cared for. But this Passover seemed to have something different about it, as they all knew; it was all around them, in the air and even in Roxanne. Like there was something else that needed to happen, something that was still to be accomplished. Veronica and Josiah both noticed that Roxanne wasn't much interested in playing anymore. She would eat alright to stay strong and healthy, but when they were out selling the cloths at the carts they set up, she would just sit there facing the direction of the city Gates, where everyone would enter and leave the city, and sniff the air and watch. Finally after days of her doing this, Veronica could no longer take it anymore. What does she wait for? She asked her uncle worriedly. I do not know child. Josiah said. I suppose she waits for Petros and Rebecca to return. No uncle, Veronica added, I feel it is something more, she sat down beside Roxanne, and placed her in her lap. You see, her eyes never leave the direction of the gates; I believe she is waiting for some sort of sign. "A sign?" Josiah exclaimed, wiping his face with a piece of the cloth they were selling, as the sun was going down but the air was still very warm. Josiah took a small break and sat down beside Veronica and Roxanne. Now Veronica he said, just exactly what kind of sign do you think she is waiting for? And from who is this sign coming from? Veronica looked at her uncle, realizing that he was quite amused at her expense! She put Roxanne back on the ground, and stood up very purposely and with all her 4.6 inches in height, she held her hand out as if to scold him and stated very matter of factly, "well uncle surely we would not know what sign it was she was waiting for.

Only Roxanne and the one sending the sign would know that"! Then she turned and walked swiftly away down the road. Josiah called after her trying not to laugh, "Veronica dear, I was just teasing you"! But she just kept on walking, and Josiah sat back down, well, what got her so excited, huh Roxanne! Roxanne! Humph, women he muttered as he got up and turned he attention back to the business of the cloth. Roxanne however never once looked away from the direction of those gates, not even when Josiah was talking to her; all she did was wait, hope and sniff the air.

The night arrives swiftly, and the fire dies low, he tries to get up off of his mat, that he had made out of palm branches and twine, Adam had made the same way the he had made once before, for Simeon, only this time he had learned a few more tricks, so this mat was put together a little sturdier, more twine and palm leaves, more sticks. Adam tried again to get up and throw some more pieces of sticks into the fire. With all the strength he had left he managed to get a few small pieces into the fire. Exhausted, Adam fell back and laid there, every breath, a hope that it was his last, he had given up. He had not eaten in days nor had anything to drink, and the pain and despair had overwhelmed him. There was just no more fight left in him. So he laid their waiting, staring at the fire by night and the light of the cave entrance by day, just waiting and hoping for death to come and release him from all the hurt of his disease and the hurt of all that he had lost. Trying to close what was left of his eyelids Adam fell back asleep, always thinking that maybe this is the last time that he would just drift off in his sleep and he wouldn't have to awake to any more pain and stench. Please God, he whispers if you are out there and you are truly a loving God, let this be my last night of pain, I beg you.

Roxanne woke with a start, hearing voices outside the window where her and Veronica were sleeping. It was nearly morning, and the entire household was still fast asleep. The air was thick with anticipation, there was something different about today, Roxanne could sense it. She jumped down off the bed and went to the window to see who the voices that she was hearing belonged to and to once again smell the air. There were two men in the road over at the house across from Josiah's. They were untying a burrow and whispering to each other! Well those are two humans who are up to no good, Roxanne started her low growl! Then a third man called out to the other two who were untying the burrow "hey what are you two doing over there to that burrow"! Well now she knew that they were up to no good, so her low growl grew into a louder more menacing one, with a bark or two thrown in for good measure! The master has need of it, one of the men replied to the third man under Roxanne's window. And that was all the third man needed to hear because he never said another word of protest after that! But Roxanne did not understand, so she kept up her protest as the two men turned and started to leave with the burrow towards the city gates. The farther they went the louder Roxanne got, finally gentle hands took hold of her and took her back to the bed, talking excitedly to her all the way back. Oh, Roxanne, Veronica cried, did you hear what they said? The master is here again, he's coming back! Everything will be just as it should, Veronica jumped out of bed, come we must get ready, I want to go early, the streets will be crowded and I want to be close to him, to honor him. I am sure Uncle Josiah will let me take you along, that is if you want to go. Without hesitation, Roxanne began to bark furiously, she knew she must follow Veronica, where or why she did not know yet, but every instinct in her said she must go out to that road today! Veronica was dressed and waiting for Josiah in the kitchen with Roxanne in her lap by the time he got up to start his day. He just stood there, looking at Veronica and Roxanne sitting in a chair, their eyes saying more than their mouth ever could. Ok, what's on your mind, Josiah said as he sat down on the chair next to them, the masters coming back to the city today. Yes, Josiah said I heard this, seems a lot of people are going to the streets to greet and welcome him. It will be a great time to sell the cloths don't you think? Josiah asked with a twinkle in his eyes as he waited for Veronica's comment, knowing full well that she wanted to go down and wait with all the others to welcome the master back into the city. Veronica respected and loved her uncle very much, and would never go against his wishes, so she just took a deep breath, trying not to let the disappointment well up in her voice, she answered, "yes uncle I suppose it would be a very good day for cloth selling. Would you like me to prepare the cart, and get the other workers ready so we can get an early start today? Unlike

Veronica, Roxanne couldn't hide her disappointment; she let out a small but very distinct and disapproving growl. Josiah smiled; well he said I think I would like you to do something else instead that is if Roxanne is ok with it! Yes, Veronica's eyes lit up a little. Josiah walked over to the front door and opened it. I would like you to find a place down that road, a safe place he added, and wait for the Masters return, to welcome him back properly. Oh, thank you Uncle, was all Veronica could say before she ran out the door after Roxanne, who was already halfway down the steps, and Josiah yelling after them, remember Veronica, a safe spot, and keep your eyes on Roxanne! I promised Petros and Rebecca we would take good care of her so keep her safe ok! I will, I promise was all he could hear as he was the two of them disappearing down the winding dirt road. So their they went, Veronica walking as fast as a lady is allowed to, and still look respectable, and Roxanne, well she had no problem keeping up with her friend, even with her limp! She just knew that something was needed of her this day, and she fully intended to be where she needed to be to accomplish whatever it was that haunted her.

# PART NINTEEN; WAITING

He laid there, in the darkness, on his bed, the fire just a small glow of embers now, and with nothing left in him to be able to even throw anything on it to encourage anymore heat, besides that it was just too painful to move anymore. Adam had given in and given up, so he just laid there and waited for death, sweet death to come and take away all the hurt, not just the psychical hurt but the hurt of losing a family that he had for such a short time, the hurt of losing Simeon, his mom and dad, Lydia, Roxanne, all of it, and what hurt most of all, was that he never could understand why! What was the point of his life, for what purpose was it all for, to just die alone, suffering? Adam couldn't think anymore, he just couldn't, he tried to turn himself to the mouth of the cave so he could look at the stars while he waited for death. Finally, after enduring immense pain and with great difficulty he managed to do this, please God he whispered if you do exist, I beg you there is nothing left for me here. I want to die, please let me die. As the embers of the fire got dimmer, so did Adam's soul, as he laid there watching the sky and the glow of the stars fade when the light of dawn started to break thru the horizon. Waiting, just waiting, was all that he could do now, all he needed to do was welcoming the sweet nothingness of death.

Come on Roxanne, hurry! Veronica shouted, as she ran down the street. I want to get as close to the road as I can, so I can wave the Palm leaves I brought and maybe even be able to touch the Master as he goes by! So hurry! I promised Uncle Josiah that I would keep a close eye on you, there will be a lot of people there, so stay very close to me ok. Roxanne barked excitedly, running to catch up with Veronica, determined to take all of it in, every instinct she was created with was telling her that her Adam was in trouble and that he needed her, where he was or how she was supposed to help, she had no idea, but she was determined to find out no matter how scary it was out there with all those human ones around. Look Roxanne, Veronica said as she pointed, there just inside the gates, that's the perfect spot and no one's there yet! As they got closer to the spot Veronica chose, they could see it was the best place, because from there they could see inside and outside the city and know sooner when the Master was getting close." Here's a branch for you to hold in your mouth", Veronica said as she gave Roxanne a small palm leaf to carry in her mouth. Then she laid down a blanket on the ground and her and Roxanne sat and waited, looking up at the fading stars and beautiful early morning sky. Suddenly Veronica stood up and wrinkled up and covered her nose, at the same time Roxanne got to her paws and started a low growl. What's that girl? Veronica said thru her hand as she covered her nose. Do you smell it too? It's the smell of death a voice softly said from behind them, startling them both, for it was still barley dawn and difficult to see. Who are you! Veronica said, frightened as she turned towards the voice. Do not be afraid, it is your friend, Mary I have come to watch over you at your Uncle's request. Mary, is it really you? Veronica asked as she tried to focus thru the haziness of early morning light. Then as Mary came closer and came into view, much to Veronica's relief she could see her lovely face smiling at her, and she gave her a hug. Mary, you gave me such a scare for a moment, Veronica said, but I'm so glad to see you, Shalom. Although you do realize that I am well capable of caring for myself and Roxanne, I fear my uncle still thinks of me as a child! Well, Mary replied, the city's streets are not as safe as you think and besides, I want to welcome the Master also. Where is your brother and sister? Veronica asked. Are they in the city also? No, Mary replied, Martha still had some cleaning to finish so Lazarus stayed with her to bring her to the city later. Veronica was silent for a moment, then she looked at Mary, may I ask, how is your brother feeling?" I mean" she stammered over her words, since all that he has been thru has happened. Mary let out a laugh, do you mean since now that he is alive again? Veronica shook her head. Why he is just wonderful! Veronica said smiling and waving her arms, "he's full of peace and joy, much more focused on the important things in life now". "Important things"? Veronica asked." Yes, you know, family friends love and most important our Creator"! Just then Roxanne gave a loud bark! Oh yes Roxanne, Mary said you are covered under family! As they were laughing at Roxanne's expense, a gust of wind came their way and with it came that awful stench. Oh, Veronica said covering her face with her head veil, that is just awful, what did you say that was again Mary, the smell of death? Yes, Mary replied if you could see farther down the road, outside the gates and before the Mount of Olives, there are some people that are also waiting for the Master's arrival. Why do they wait out there? Veronica asked. Why not inside here? They are unclean. Mary replied. Unclean? Veronica asked. Yes, diseased, they are outcasts, not allowed in the city, and if you get near them or touch them, you also will become like them and have to leave the city, forever banned from your life here and your loved ones! Veronica turned towards the entrance to the city and the source of the smell; they wait for healing from the Master, don't they. Yes, Mary replied. And will he? Heal them I mean, asked Veronica. Mary walked over to Veronica and looked her in the eyes, the Master is kind and loves all, and if you truly believe he is who he says he is, and that he was sent by God the Father, then yes he will heal. I pray that they believe and that he touches all of them and makes them whole again, so they don't have to hurt anymore, Veronica said with her eyes filling up with tears. Well, Mary said as she wrapped her arms around her young friend, why don't we pray for that together, ok, while we wait for the rising of the sun! Roxanne sat and listened to them both, trying to understand all that was being said. She sniffed the cool morning air desperately trying to realize just what it was she needed to do. She did understand when she heard the Master's name for he had held her, and she had never felt such a peace or such a connection as she did with him. Then something happened, as she sat on that blanket and sniffed the cool morning air, smelling that awful yet familiar stench, and hearing of those people beyond the city's walls, started to give Roxanne memories of Adam and how he had cared for Simeon. Then that led to a memory of a smell, that same awful smell that she smells now, and a sore on a leg, but whose leg? A gentle breeze came by and Roxanne was surrounded by the smell which triggered her memory, all of a sudden she realized that it was Adam's leg that had that sore and that same smell that she smells now! She remembered running away from him because of this same smell ; faint as it was then, it was the same awful stench, she just knew it! That cave! The scary noise, the poke, it all was starting to make sense to her now! Roxanne began to bark, loudly and furiously, at Veronica and Mary, pulling with her teeth at Veronica's clothes, trying to communicate that she needed to go outside of these walls, and she needed to leave now! But Veronica could not understand, so she just kept telling her to be quiet which only caused Roxanne to pull harder, and then bark louder! Finally Veronica picked her up, what is the matter, she said sternly! Why are you acting so badly? I'm sorry Mary, she is usually so well behaved, said Veronica as she apologized and continued to hold on to Roxanne. Seems like she is trying to tell you something, replied Mary. Here, give her to me, maybe I can find out what's wrong. Mary took Roxanne from Veronica's arms, and looked at her face, into her eyes. Then she whispered something in her ear, untied the small rope that was around her waist, which other end was still being held by Veronica, and then proceeded to set her on the ground, free from her rope that kept her bound. Roxanne looked up at Mary as she squatted down and said, "Go ahead girl, do what you must, then come back home!" Roxanne licked Mary on the cheek, and gave her a quiet bark, turned and ran off, out of the city's gates and down the long dirt road, just as fast as her small injured but powerful legs could carry her! Turning and noticing that Roxanne was gone, Veronica shouted angrily at Mary, "Why did you do that"! I promised that I would not let any harm come to her! Come on, we have to go and get her back! Mary took hold of Veronica's hand holding her back, "No" she said. "Let her go, she knows what she must do"! But my Uncle will be furious with me Veronica protested. Veronica! Mary said sternly as she turned her friend so that they face to face! "Listen to me; everything will be fine, Roxanne will return"! How can you know that Mary? Veronica asked, tears welling up in her eyes. Mary's face softened and she smiled, she looked up to the sky, now beginning to show its full light of morning. The sun will be full soon and the streets will be thick with people soon, why don't you go and get your uncle, tell him what has happened, and bring him back here. I will wait here, in case Roxanne returns before you return, ok. He's going to be very angry with me, Veronica said with some strain in her voice. Well, get him anyway

Mary replied, surely he won't be showing much anger with the Master coming into the city this way soon! True, Veronica smiled. Ok I'll be right back, as fast as I can, I don't want to miss seeing him either! So off she went, down the dirty streets of the city, as fast as her two legs would carry her!

# PART TWENTY; COURAGE

Darkness filled his cave, his mind and his spirit; he could barely take a breath without some part of his body crying out in painful protest! As he lay there, curled up in a ball, his tattered clothes stuck to his open wounds seeping infection and bloody serum. He was only able now to close one eye, for the other eyelid had been eaten away by his disease and the infection it created. All Adam wanted now still was death, and death was what was very, very close now.

She came to dead stop; looking into the dark hole of the cave's entrance, afraid to go any farther, Roxanne listened for that awful noise that she had heard here before. Then she gave a loud cry, and smelled the air and that same stench filled her nostrils, determined not to let anything intimidate her and driven by her love for her Adam, and if that's what it took to find her master, then so be it, so into the darkness she went! Slowly at first, then with her teeth bared and growling, as she walked into the dark cave not knowing what she would encounter once inside.

What was that noise? Adam tried to listen, did I hear something or is my mind playing tricks on me. He couldn't be sure, wait there it is again! It's like a low growl, maybe it's a lion, and he's come to eat me, he thought. No, not even a very hungry Lion could stand to be near me, much less eat me, Adam said to himself. Then he felt it! Faint at first, breath on his neck, behind him! Adam braced himself. He could no longer turn his neck, he was too weak to move his body and his speech was barely above a whisper. So he just laid there waiting for that ferocious beast behind him, welcoming those sharp teeth and claws, to finish doing what this horrible disease was taking so long to do. Closing his one eye, he waited...

Roxanne, growling stopped suddenly as she came upon something in the darkness. As she approached it, she sniffed the object before her. At once that familiar, putrid smell filled her nostrils, but with much more intensity than ever before, but there was another scent present, this one was very faint but it was much more familiar to her than the rotten one! Roxanne forced herself to move closer to the lump, sniffing again the faint scent of familiarity a little deeper, as it grew stronger in her mind she suddenly remember what that smell reminded her of! That smell, it was her Adam! She had found him! But why was he not moving? Calling her name? Taking her into his arms and holding her? Confused, Roxanne stepped back and sat, whimpering. It smelled like him, but it didn't act like him. Standing, she bristled the fur on her back, and she walked around the lump to the front of it, see its eyes! Then I can tell, if it's truly my Adam or not! Growling lowly, Roxanne starts to go to the other side of the lump, slowly she approaches, ready at any moment to strike back, should this not be her Adam, but an imposter out to fool or hurt her! As she approached the front of the lump, still very aware of the two scents, the horrible one and the smell that reminded her of Adam, which was fast getting stronger .In the darkness of the cave, and the contrast of the dying fire with its glowing embers now helped Roxanne eyes to focus on the partial face before her. As she looked at the lump's face, she could not see the eyes, one was closed, the other hidden in the darkness. So she moved a little closer, still trying to focus on the face. Adam could feel the beast's breath on his face, he laid there, waiting for the first penetrating bite, trying not to open his eye, not wanting to see the snarly face, the sharp teeth that would be the final cause of his death, he didn't want that to be the last thing on his mind before he died. So he closed his one eye, and tried to hide the other in the mat's blanket, he felt hot breath on his face, and listened to that awful snarled growl come closer and closer! Then he felt it! But it wasn't something that he was expecting; it was something that he hadn't felt in such a long time! Something wet and slimy went across what was the only normal part left on his face that has not been affected by the disease, his ear and part of his cheek right next to it! Adam could not help but open up his eye, and what he saw was even more disbelieving! It wasn't a mean lion that had come to eat him, but it was just a little dog there before him! And not just any old dog, it was his dog, his Roxanne! Here, right in front of him! Oh to see her there, to feel her licking his ear, almost gave Adam the strength to sit up, but all he could do was try and smile and whisper her name, "Roxanne", you found me, you found me". "I'm so sorry for leaving you girl, I didn't want you to see me like this, but I'm so glad that you found me, I don't want to die out here all alone!" I can't believe you found me, I love you girl, thank you for finding me. Then Adam could no longer stay awake, he fell into a deep yet more peaceful sleep, knowing at least now that he would not die alone! Roxanne laid down next to her beloved Adam, very tired from all the running and excitement, even though the sun was starting to peek over the horizon, warming the air, it was still a cold morning, so Roxanne snuggled close, still confused as to why he left her and why he was here. What more was there to do? Why doesn't he just get up and they go home? What were they waiting for? Roxanne fell into a restless sleep surrounded by such familiar scents and the cave that they all once lived in with Simeon, sparked pictures in her mind of how he looked right before Adam took him away and put him in the ground next to her mama. She woke up with suddenly, understanding now just what was happening to her Adam! Well, she would not just sit here and do nothing and watch him leave her again! Fearfully she started whimpering and licking his ear trying to wake him, but he did not move. So she tried to nudge him with her head, nothing. Getting more frightened and confused at the lack of response from Adam she wasn't sure what else to do. Then she heard voices outside of the cave, she ran towards the mouth of the cave, not seeing anything, she went a little farther out and looked in the direction of the city. Then she saw him, riding on a burrow, with a small group of people following, and heading towards the city, was the one who found and held her that day in the city and caused her feel so at peace and loved. That's it Roxanne concluded, he is the answer! He would know what to do, he healed Rebecca's eyes, I seen it, and if I can get him up here he can heal my Adam too! So Roxanne began to bark, loud and excitely, trying to get the attention from anyone who was down there with him! Especially hoping to get the attention of the Master! As she barked louder and louder, wanting anyone to look up, she walked down a little more, reluctant to leave Adam alone much longer, she barked as loud as she could over and over, but no one looked up and no one could hear her, the crowd cheering for the Savior was just too loud! Well then if she couldn't get the master to Adam, then she would just have to get Adam to the Master!! Running back to the cave, Roxanne grabbed Adam by the sleeve, pulling and barking trying to get him up, to move, to go and see the Master, but all Adam could do was open his eye and whisper, "No Roxanne, it's too late". "Please, just let me hold you when I die, then you can go, ok". Adam tried to reach for Roxanne to hold her, but she moved too fast, and he move very,, very slowly, his thin pale, sore eaten arm just catching the air as he tried to grasped tried to grasp her with the few fingers that he had left on his hand. Sensing that she had precious little time left, Roxanne excitedly ran around the cave trying to find something, anything, to help get Adam down to where she needed him to be. Just as she was starting to lose hope, the sun's rays shined upon the front part of where Adam was laying, causing Roxanne to look in that direction, turning her head sideways, wondering what it was she saw, and noticing something sticking out from under Adam's head. Curious she went over to investigate, sniffing and pawing at it Roxanne could see that it was some kind of round stick, and attached to that was something that was under Adam. Roxanne put the stick in her mouth, careful not to bite down too hard. As she gave the stick a gentle tug, and to her surprise, it moved! Not only did the stick move but the thing under move too which also caused her Adam to move! Startled by the jolt of the moving mat Adam whispered his protest, but Roxanne was jumping and barking so loudly his voice was not heard. Quickly she looked around for a cover for Adam, finding one against the cave wall, grabbing it she carried it over to Adam and tried her best to cover him completely, head to feet. Adam thinking of course that Roxanne could no longer stand to smell or look at him anymore Adam tried to help, ok girl he said softly, I'll cover myself, if you promise not to leave me. After he was all covered Roxanne gave another loud bark, and went to the cave entrance to make sure that the master was still there. He was, he had actually stopped a ways before the city gates, almost like he was waiting for someone or something. Quickly, she went and got a hold of the stick and tugged at it, this time with more power and determination than before. The mat moved quite easily considering that it was somewhat larger and heavier than Roxanne herself! But it was quite sturdy, with sticks intertwining on the bottom; palm leaves on the top, covered by a piece of purple cloth that Adam had saved, a gift from Lydia. As she moved him from the cave's darkness into the light of the sun, he jerked with pain, he tried to look out from under the blanket, to see what she was doing, but the light was just too bright for his eyes and without the cover, the cool morning air and the sun rays would cause too much pain for him to bear, so he just laid there, curled up into a ball, holding on to the corner of the cloth, and whispering over and over, " please, please it's too late, give up, just stop". But giving up or stopping was the furthest thing from Roxanne's mind! As she pulled with her mouth, she would feel the trail down with her hind legs, finding that her lame leg in front would cause her to have to stop every so often for the pain to subside. Thankfully the dirt road wasn't very steep and it was a well-used road so there were not very many time that she needed to stop and rest, she knew that she didn't have a lot of time to waste, Adam was barley holding on. Now and then she would glance towards where the Master was to make sure he wasn't gone. Roxanne found that getting thru the bumpy cave entrance and thru the first fifty feet proved to be the most difficult, aster that the road was smoother. Fearful that her Adam wasn't going to be alive much longer, Roxanne stopped only once more to check and see if the Master was still there, and to her delight, he hadn't moved at all, he was still in the same spot, on a hill overlooking the city, waiting or something, she didn't care which, she just knew if she kept up she would be down there before he entered the city, just in front of the gates. So she pulled, and pulled and pulled some more, until her mouth was sore and bleeding, until her paws were raw and pleading, her neck and back crying out in pain, telling her to quit with every move she made. But she could not, she loved Adam too much to give up now, what happened to her didn't matter; all that mattered was getting her master to the healer in time! And she Roxanne for whatever reason was given this task to do alone! She would not fail her Adam, no matter which part of her body cried out in protest, she just wouldn't! The closer she got to the city the weaker he got, and the less protest he made, which only caused Roxanne to go even faster. When she arrived at the place where the people started to gather, things proved to become a bit more difficult. A little dog pulling something on a mat was an interesting sight, but not interesting enough to make a path to the front of the dirt road, where he was going to pass by soon! So getting through the crowd, was harder than she anticipated, oh sure she tried the usual, barking, growling thing. She even tried to do a trick or two, but not enough people would notice or get out of the way. Just as she was beginning to feel defeated, a strong wind came up and blew just enough cover off of Adam to expose his open sored, puss filled, three fingered hand and arm, and of course along with that came the awful smell! Well, that certainly got their attention! Practically every eye that was in that general area turned around and placed itself on Roxanne and Adam all staring at them in disbelief and holding their clothes to their faces! For a brief moment, Roxanne froze afraid to move, then she remembered why she was there, and how much her Adam meant to her, she gave a low growl, lifted her head high, left Adam's arm exposed and went back to the business of getting him to the front of that crowd, which now was quite easy, since no one wanted anything to do with either of them, they stood far away on both sides making a pathway, right to the front of the dirt road, and to the Masters help! All you could hear as she pulled Adam along was the scraping of his mat along the road, from the back to the front trying to go as fast as her little legs would carry both of them, without any help from anyone else nearby! Finally she had arrived to her destination, now all she had to do was watch and wait for him. Surely, the Master would not act like these others, so she sat down by Adam, exhausted, not daring to lay down or close her eyes. Afraid that she would miss the arrival of him passing by, so waiting was all that was left for either of them to do now. For Adam, well he was waiting to die, but for Roxanne, she was waiting for him to live!

Teacher, look! A man cried as he pointed towards the city. "People are lining up on either side of the road, all the way into the city to welcome you"! Shall we go now, he added. "I guess the one that you were waiting for is not going to show" another man said. Jesus looked at all his friends and smiled. The one who I was waiting on is indeed here! He replied. They all looked around confused, but Master, we have all been with you here all day! No one new has arrived! The Master stood and smiled again, saying simply "she has gone ahead of us, come lets go greet her and all of my brothers and sisters"! The Healers friends did not understand his words and looked confusingly at each other not knowing who he was speaking of, they just shrugged their shoulders and went over to hold the burrow's rope, so Jesus could once again begin his entrance into the Great city' which was flocked with people waiting to welcome their king! A city which dirt roads were lined on both sides with people waving palm branches and singing, and next to its magnificent gates was one very hopeful little dog!

# PART TWENTY ONE; FULL CIRCLE

Come quickly Uncle, Veronica yelled as she ran up to the cart full of cloth, something terrible has happened! Her face stained with tears, her hair full of sweat! What's wrong my dear? Josiah said looking very worried. I'm so sorry, I tried to stop her, but she said it was necessary, and now she's gone, and I don't know where! Oh please, please forgive me, she just kept saying. Veronica! Josiah said sternly as he took her by the shoulders trying to calm her. "Calm down, take a deep breath and try to explain what is wrong, slowly"! Veronica took a deep breath, then began again, Mary the one you sent out to watch Roxanne and I is out there near the gates, she told me to come and get you. She said that you needed to go out there, that there was something that you needed to be there for. What, Josiah protested, does the woman realize that I am very busy here! That I promised Petros to manage his cloth selling? After all there's only a few more days left until Passover, it's the busiest time,, I can't just leave it to my helpers! Did you explain that's the reason why I let you and Roxanne go there alone? Yes, uncle I did, right before she whispered something in Roxanne's ear, and then…Veronica hesitated. Then what! Josiah said a bit more harshly than he intended. Well, Veronica said, and then she let her go out the city gates. Whaaat! Josiah yelled. She did what! I'm sorry, she said that Roxanne had something she needed to do. You bet she does, like get run over or killed, Josiah started in again, oh my, my I promised Petros to keep her safe, till they came back for her. What am I going to do now! He walked back and forth worrying and talking to himself. Uncle! Veronica got his attention, come with me, she pulled on his sleeve, please; Mary said that we must hurry. I am sure that the Master will know what to do anyway, hurry so we don't to miss his arrival! Josiah looked at his helpers, go they said we'll be fine, we will take care of everything here, with that the two of them hurried down the road towards what they thought was a very long, long day of dog searching!

Hosanna! Hosanna! The crowd was loud, Adam listened. Are those angels? He wondered. Am I dead? Trying now to open his eye and seeing only slight light, Adam wasn't sure if he was truly dead or just slightly alive! So he tried to move and the pain brought him quickly back to reality, causing him to cry out, which caused Roxanne to panic and start barking furiously again, which caused again the crowd to draw their attention to her until someone in the crowd yelled, "look here he comes"! That was all it took of course to cause a flood of people to move closer to the road, singing and yelling all trying to get the attention of the King! Roxanne upon seeing the master approaching grabbed the stick again and pulled with all her might, trying to get Adam as close as possible, but there were so many people around now, how could he possible notice one little dog and one sick man? What could she do to get his attention, especially when so many of these humans, were wanting to do the same thing? Well, whatever it was it had better be quick or else he would be past her and she would have lost her Adam's only chance, so she did the only thing she could think to do, using her mouth Roxanne totally removed the cloth that was covering Adam, exposing his entire pus-filled open sored raw part of his body to the light, and in turn exposing the entire crowd to her Adam! Well, it didn't take very long for the gasps and stares to begin, then next came the clothes over the faces and noses and of course the moving far away from them! And that was exactly what Roxanne was hoping for! Now all she had to do was sit next to him and bare her teeth, hoping that no one would call her bluff and throw both of them out of the city, and away from the Healer's hand. No one did, not one single solitary person moved close to her or Adam, either to help or to harm. So Roxanne decided to make her move, grabbing the stick she started to pull Adam towards the middle of the road, right where she was sure that the Master could not miss seeing them! With every scrape of the wood along the dirt road, Adam exposed, would beg Roxanne to stop, but she wouldn't listen; nothing would stop her now, for she knew this is what she had been waiting for! This was the reason why she was left here, and she would see it to the end! She finally made it to the middle, right in the path of the burrow the Master was riding, and there he was, just ahead! The people on either side of the road just watched her and Adam, their mouths covered, eyes wide with fear, but all around and behind the Healer were many, many people shouting and dancing! Afraid that the Master would not notice Adam or that the burrow would just trample over him, Roxanne walked out in front of Adam, and just stood there, as tall as she could. Her head and tail held high! Waiting, either she would be noticed by the Master or die with her Adam; she had done all that she could now and waited for her fate to come closer!

Mary! Mary! Veronica cried as she and Josiah quickly approached her. "Have you found Roxanne yet"? Mary calmly turned towards them saying, "Josiah, how good to see you again, then she turned to Veronica and seeing how distraught she looked, she leaned over and kissed her cheek, then whispered into her ear as she pointed down the street to the middle of the road, "don't worry Veronica, Roxanne is safe and she is right over there"! Veronica's eyes followed where Mary's finger was pointing, causing Josiah to do the same, seeing it, but their minds not believing the scene before them. Oh no Veronica cried what is she doing? If she doesn't move she will get hurt by the burrow or the crowd, and what is it that she seem to be protecting behind her! As they moved to go get Roxanne out of harm's way they were stopped by Mary's arm. No, do not interfere! But, Veronica protested, she will get killed! The Master is near, he will not let any harm come to either of them! What do you mean either of them? Veronica asked. Is that actually a person with her in the road? Come, see for yourselves she answered, and lets go welcome our King back home! So Josiah, Mary and Veronica made their way closer to their King, to Roxanne and to what they suppose was a person laying in the road behind Roxanne.

Lord, the crowd is getting very loud and crowded! I'm afraid that they will crush us! One of the Masters followers cried as he led the burrow down the dusty street, heading toward the city's gates, joyous that so many came out to welcome them, yet afraid at the same time! Why do you fear? The Teacher said, this is a day of joy! Be happy for I am only here for a short while longer. Look! Someone shouted as they pointed down the road, just ahead, in the middle of the road, there is something blocking in our path! As they got closer they realized that it was a dog, standing there with something or someone behind it. I suppose the dog will get out of the way if we just keep moving towards it, the follower who was leading the burrow down the road said. Jesus just smiled and said nothing. But Roxanne did not move as the follower had thought she would, in face the closer they got the more she stood tall, until the man pulling the burrow and even the burrow's hoofs were now just a few feet from Roxanne's body and yet she still didn't budge! Thinking he would just push the dog out of the way, Peter stopped in his tracks when he caught sight of the mass of flesh that used to be a human, laying there behind that dog, covering his face instantly with his cloak and immediately trying to turn the burrow around quickly to get his Rabbi out of there as fast as possible, all the while yelling," there is an unclean sinner in the road, beware"! He turned to the other followers, he yelled" we must protect the Master, turn away quickly"! But as burrows will be the more he tried to turn the beast the more stubborn he became and didn't budge! As fear started to take hold of the people, and panic took over their minds, and just as they were ready to run away, the Healer raised his hand and a in a calm quiet voice he said, "Be at peace", "do not fear". With all eyes on him he got down off the burrow, immediately the burrow moved aside and allowed him access to the disturbing scene before him. Upon seeing the Healer before her Roxanne instantly stopped her threating stance and snarling, she walked over to him and lay at his feet, licking at his feet and crying. He bent down, picked her up and cradled her in his arms as he told her in a quiet voice," Roxanne, you have completed your task well, you brought him where he must be!, Now it is up to him little one", as he walked over to Adam, Jesus placed Roxanne on the ground next to him. Bending down he looked upon the mass of flesh that lay upon that mat with great compassion, the mass of flesh trying to cover his face with his gnarled hand. Then he stood up again and looked around at the crowd, with their faces covered by their clothes, a look of horror upon their faces and in their eyes, and he took pity upon them, because of their ignorance and lack of understanding. After all this time with me and you still do not understand why my Father sent me. This man's illness was not caused by his sins or by his father's sins. This man needs your compassion, not your judgment! For this reason I came, not to condemn but to forgive! The Master turned to his closest friends, who also had their faces covered, and asked," did I not just give a new command? "To love one another as I have loved you"? Having said this, they all lowered their eyes, Jesus turned his attention once again to Adam and Roxanne. Bending down he whispered close to Adam's ear, calling his name, but Adam didn't move, Jesus took his sore filled three fingered hand into his own and called his name again, "Adam" he said this time louder. Adam's one eye opened and a very weak yes came out of very swollen very dry lips. Adam, your Roxanne loves you very much she wants you to live and be healed, Jesus bend down lower, so they were face to face, "what do you want Adam" ? He asked knowing full well what was about to take place. Adam tried to focus on the face before him, and then he saw them, those eyes, and he remembered the young man in the street so long ago that day that Roxanne had gotten run over and how he touched her and healed her, this man he had those same eyes! I,I want to Live! He whispered with all that he had left in him. Jesus smiled and stood up holding out his hand he said, "then believe and live'! Instantly, Adam could feel the pain start to leave his body, starting with his toes and working slowly up his feet, then his legs, knees, stomach, arms—as the pain left it was being replaced by an incredible rushing of warmth and overwhelming peace inside that was so indescribable to Adam that all he could do was just lay there speechless and wait for this miracle to overtake and heal his whole being from the inside and out. Of course this took mere seconds but to Adam it felt like an eternity of pain and helplessness was being removed, it was Roxanne's barking and face licking that brought him back to clarity! He actually could feel her wet cool tongue all over on his face and see her now so clearly, Laughing he suddenly sat up, causing the crowd to gasp in astonishment as to what the beheld before them, not even believing their own eyes! Picking up Roxanne, Adam stares in disbelief at his hand before him, his five fingered perfect hand! Then that perfect hand touches two perfect legs and moves up to touch a perfect face all covered with skin as soft as a newborn baby's ! Adam looks up and sees another perfect hand being held out in front of him, it is the hand of his Healer, there waiting, ready to help him stand up again! He sets Roxanne down and takes that hand planting his feet firmly down, he tries to stand for the first time in weeks! Grateful and joyful Adam hugs his healer thanking him over and over; he glances over to his companions to the one holding the burrow that Jesus was riding, when something familiar catches his eye! He slowly walks over to the burrow not quite used to his new found legs yet, standing next him was Jesus along with many who followed him curious at touching the walking miracle, and of course Roxanne, next to her a very relived Josiah, Mary and Veronica grateful to have Roxanne back in her sights! The Master stood behind Adam as he just stared at the burrow's back. What do you see? The master asked Adam. That blanket, there one the burrow's back? May I see it? Adam asked. The man holding the burrow handed the blanked to Adam, who then saw the embroidered writing, "FOR YOU MY SWEET BABY BOY", immediately, tears filled his eyes as he held it close to his face. Do you recognize it? The Healer asked. My mother made it for me, when I was a baby, it was all I had left of her when she died, Adam answered sadly. Then he looked up at those eyes confused, but how did you get it? He Asked his Healer. Smiling, Jesus asked, do you remember what happened to the blanket? Adam thought back, to when he was a small boy living in the streets, after the death of his parents. Well he said thoughtfully, I used to keep it folded and inside my shirt, next to my heart. I remember there was this family, who was living in a stable, they had just had a baby, and one very cold night they saw me standing outside and invited me in, back then, even as young as I was, I was already starting to become pretty angry at the world, but I knew if I didn't get somewhere warm I would freeze. They shared with me what little they had to eat and let me hold their baby boy, Adam smiled, I remember thinking how nice it would have been to have a baby brother. Anyway he continued, the next morning they said they were leaving, to go to Egypt, asked me to go with them, but I lied, said I was waiting for my family to come for me, my foolish pride was alive and well, even at that young age I guess, he added blushing slightly. Well, he continued I noticed that sweet little baby lying there in that feeding stall wrapped in rags, I realized that they had nothing warm to wrap him in, so before they left I took my blue blanked out from under my shirt, and wrapped it around the baby, to keep him warm. But I still don't understand how you ended up with…… Adams eyes met Jesus eyes and he finally realized the truth! You are the baby that I wrapped my blanket in! He said with excitement. Yes! The Healer said with a smile. You gave me your last possession and your most loved possession just to keep me warm, and now my sweet child, not only do I give you your health back I give you, he looked around, I give all of you, my life, my truth, and my peace! Adam fell to his face before Jesus, crying and thanking him, looking up he asked, "Lord, what do you mean when you say, you give us your life"? The Healer once again leaned down his arms to Adam to help him arise. Well that's all the invitation Roxanne needed She leapt into his arms nearly knocking him over, so grateful for all that he had done for her master, causing the whole crowd around to burst out in laughter! Jesus held out a hand to Adam, come he said the answer to your question is not for you to know now, one will come to you later on, believe in what he tells you, because he tells you on my authority! Adam looked into those eyes, not understanding what he had meant but accepting his answer anyway. Then Lord, Adam replied, what can I do now for you, to repay you for giving me back my life? Jesus looked at Adam his eye full of love, he told him "there is nothing you or anyone could do to redeem yourself Adam, just believe in me and what I have told you, and I will accomplish what is needed to make all things new! Like his beautiful soft new skin! Veronica blurted out, as she felt Adams face and arms. Jesus smiled, but said nothing more. One of his disciples, who Jesus seemed to love a great deal, spoke up saying, Rabbi the crowd in the city is getting restless waiting for you, should we proceed into the city now? Yes! Adam said, let's go and tell all what he has done for me, so that they will know that what he speaks is the truth and that they too can believe and live! As Adam started for the city gates the Healer touched his arm and spoke, "Adam wait"! Immediately Adam stopped and turned asking," yes Rabbi what is it, what is the matter? Your future is not within these city walls, your destiny lies outside there. He said this as he pointed out away from the city. There is someone who you need to see, he continued, someone who is still hurting very badly at your leaving, and only to actually to see and touch you will bring about the healing.

Adam looked at his Savior, his heart breaking, but I want to stay with you Lord, to be near you. He said afraid if he left his sight so would this feeling of amazing peace and joy also would leave. The healer looked Adam in his eyes and kindly patiently spoke," Child, you must go, the days ahead here will be dark and full of evil, I do not wish for you to see this, your job is to go beyond this place and tell everyone, what has happened, so that they can also believe and live"! "Remember what I have said, someone will come to you and tell you of what has taken place here one day, so you will know that I am truly who I say I am! Now go in peace, he said as he handed Adam his blue blanket which had fallen onto the ground. Adam took it from him not knowing what else to say except, I will do as you say Lord even though the thought of leaving him here gave Adam a very fearful feeling deep in his soul, like something terrible was about to happen. So he folded the blanket, placed it inside his shirt, next to his heart, then he said his good-byes to Josiah, Veronica and Mary and thanked them for everything and for taking such good care of Roxanne for him. Then he turned and started to walk away down the road. Seeing him walk away from her and being in the arms of the Healer, feeling totally safe and at peace, tore Roxanne's heart in two, wanting to stay, but needing to leave. "You have been a wonderful friend to Adam, Roxanne" Jesus said, well done, you go now, and be whole! You have placed your love for him above yourself and there is not a greater gift you could have given! "Go little one, and be happy"! The Healer said as he placed Roxanne on the ground. As Adam turned to leave he knew that Roxanne was still in his Masters arms, but he could not ask for her back nor could he ask Roxanne to choose him over her Creator, so he just walked away tears filling his eyes, yet still full of joy and peace inside. Then he heard her "Bark, Bark, Bark"! Turning he saw her running to him, really running up to him and jumping she flew into his arms, knocking them both down! Roxanne! Your limp, its gone! He said as he kissed her head and laughed. He healed you too! Adam quickly stood to see if he could see their Healer, and for one brief moment their eyes met and Jesus smiled, and then he was swallowed up by the large crowd of people praising him! But Adam knew that one day he would be looking into those incredible eyes again and be able to stay with him forever.

Someday, he said out loud as he petted Roxanne, you never gave up on me did you girl, he said as he gave her a hug, "thank-you for caring for me". And now I am healed, and your limp is gone, so we are off to do as the Healer told us to do! Come Roxanne it's time to spread our story and tell others of Jesus, and guess where our first stop is? A place called Thyatira! Why you ask? I'll tell you, he said laughing, there's a certain girl there, who's very sad, the Healer had told me so, and she needs to know my story. Besides I hear she is the maker of this beautiful purple cloth! Roxanne put her paw over her face and whined! Adam laughed, loud and joyous feeling so much happiness inside that he thought he would burst if he didn't.

So down the dusty dirt road they went. A new Adam and A new Roxanne, ready for whatever adventure life had waiting for them! With no limp at all!!!

### THE END
(or is it the beginning)